EGRYN

EGRYN

Donald Rees

Matador
Unit E2 Airfield Business Park,
Harrison Road, Market Harborough,
Leicestershire. LE16 7UL
Tel: 0116 2792299
Email: books@troubador.co.uk
Web: www.troubador.co.uk/matador
Twitter: @matadorbooks

ISBN 978 1803132 457

British Library Cataloguing in Publication Data.
A catalogue record for this book is available from the British Library.

Printed and bound in Great Britain by 4edge Limited
Typeset in 11pt Minion Pro by Troubador Publishing Ltd, Leicester, UK

Matador is an imprint of Troubador Publishing Ltd

I would like to dedicate this book to my grandchildren: Iwan Rhys, Gruffydd Rhys, Gwyn Huw Tomos, Alis Hâf, Iorwerth Llywelyn, Meredydd Cadwaladr and Bronwen Eleri.

CHAPTER ONE

THIS IS US

Elves have been living in this country for hundreds of years. It's almost impossible to see them. They live in oak trees, usually very big ones. In the warm months they sleep outside on a spot where two thick branches meet, but in colder months inside the trunk. When I say sleep, I really mean go into a trance, as they just sit or lie with eyes open and appear to be awake, but are not.

One of the reasons you can't see them is that the colours of their clothes are exactly the same as the tree. Their hair is acorn colour whilst in the tree, but in sunshine it changes to the same colour as the grass. They are also very small; older ones can be as tall as 30 centimetres, but most are smaller. Some have lived to be 222 years old, then for some reason they get ill and go off to a secret place they have chosen to die. Usually it is the same place their family has been going to for hundreds of years. An elf is considered to be a child until they are 40 years old and fully grown.

For some reason their hair can grow shoulder length in one day, then can stop growing for years. Us humans wash our hair to keep it clean but elves use a powder made out of ground fern to rub in their hair, and if they then put some morning dew from the grass and stand in the sunlight, it shrinks and slowly disappears. It takes about two minutes for it to grow back to shoulder length, in perfectly clean condition. They do this every time there is a full moon.

As they've only got small snub noses they smell through their ears, which are much longer than ours and get more pointed as the years go by. You can roughly tell the age of an elf by the length of their ears. They grow upwards and don't stick out at all. Their faces hardly change as they are a happy people, don't frown or worry and even when they are very old they don't have wrinkles on their faces, which remain as smooth as a baby's bum. No elf has ever had a beard or moustache, as no hair grows on their face except for their eyebrows, which are very thin.

Most of the time their eyes are green but they can change when their mood changes. If really happy, their eyes can be yellow, and when sad they go really dark. Their faces are usually happy but as their ears are so sensitive to smell they pull a horrible face when something has a really strong pong. If for example a farmer puts silage on a field, an elf can smell it ten miles away.

For hundreds of years there was enough countryside with lots of oak woods for some elves to spend their whole lives without seeing a human. They call us "arogs" and if a human comes within 100 metres, they can smell you and hide.

However as the years have gone by the trees are disappearing; more houses and roads are being built and the number of elves in the whole of the country is less than a thousand, when there used to be tens of thousands.

A few wild elves now live in ones or twos and wander around. They haven't got a home. The wood elves are not very happy to see them as they've had contact with arogs and might bring some of their germs. Also they have their own rules. Some have been known to steal items off arogs, and they are considered to be undesirable characters. They often wear their hair in braids and somehow allow it to grow long. No ordinary elf would ever steal from another elf and they have not got anyone except the king or queen to enforce the rules. They don't need police at all. If there are any disputes, they are decided by their leader, which can be an elected king or a queen.

Some elves tried living in beech or elm trees but they became ill after a while, and so where possible would have to find an oak tree which was empty. Only one family could live in one tree. It would be an elf (male) and elfine (female) and children. When the children become 40 they like to find their own tree if available, then get a partner and then start their own family. So as oak trees are getting fewer, there are far fewer elves than there have ever been.

After about five years finding a partner, and then another five years together, two weeks before their 50th birthday (which is still young for an elf), they start their own family. Two weeks before their birthday they cut all the hair off each other's heads and mix it together in a special birthing bowl, which each family has had for hundreds of years. This hair is then sprinkled with fairy dust, which you have to get from the queen elf. The bowl is covered with a blanket woven out of spiders' webs, put inside the trunk of the oldest tree in the wood, and two weeks later when the cover is taken off, a baby elf is inside.

When they collect the dust the king hides a coloured stone in his hands and you have to pick one. One brown coloured stone for a boy, and a green one for a girl. You just touch one hand but he doesn't tell you which colour you picked, so two weeks later it's a nice surprise.

Every elf in the world has the same birthday, March the 1st. It's a special day as everyone has a party to celebrate their birthday.

The children all have names beginning with the same letter as their mother.

In this particular wood, there are about seven big oak trees close together that are old enough, therefore big enough, for a family to live in. There are a few smaller oaks if a 40-year-old wants to live alone. In one of the trees lives an elf called Egryn, who is 39-years-old and will shortly be the magic 40, and will be able to live alone in his own tree.

March the 1st is coming and the big birthday celebrations will take place, but this year it's even more special as his great grandfather Goronwy will be 222 and has decided to leave the day after his party to go to his special spot to die. It's not sad, as after a year he will be reborn and start again. He's quite looking forward to it. It's like having a very long sleep and waking up young.

"I'm fed up with these old bones, it will be nice to be young and fit again," he kept telling everyone. "I wonder if I will come back as an elf or an elfine. Don't care really."

The week before, anyone who saw him would shake his

hand and tell him they were looking forward to seeing him again, in a year's time.

Over the years, though, the woods have shrunk as arogs are moving nearer and chopping them down. There used to be trees as far as the eye could see and an elf could travel for miles without touching the ground, just going from branch to branch. There are no elves now living within 30 miles of their wood and the nearest ones, a long way away, don't like visiting as they have to cross stone roads where these metal noisy things come really fast making a "zoom zoom" noise. In fact, they are not sure if they are still there as Selwyn the spy said their site was empty the last time he visited.

Egryn has never spoken to an arog or seen one, and says he doesn't want to, but his grandfather says they are getting nearer, one day they will come to their wood and chop it down, and when he's reborn he's going to hope he's in a really big wood with hundred of elves, like it used to be.

The younger elves didn't believe him and called him a misery guts.

CHAPTER TWO

STRANGE VISITORS

The last day of February, everyone was getting ready for the big party. The elfines mainly were making the food (honey and acorn pie was Egryn's favourite), and the male elves mostly were preparing wooden gifts for everyone, and making acorn beer. Rhiannon, Egryn's friend, would be busy for weeks making new costumes. Her friend Alis Hâf would be out scouring the wood for plants, flowers and reeds to be converted by Rhiannon into costumes. She could make clothes out of anything, even stingy nettles, and they would be light and waterproof.

Egryn was hoping for a new catapult, which he wanted to use to shoot at the buzzards that flew over their woods, and could eat an elf in one gulp. Lucky they've got great hearing and can hear the buzzards swooping down with time to spare. Only birds of prey were their enemies, they would not shoot a catapult at any other living thing.

Goronwy was going around giving away his possessions as he was leaving after tomorrow's party and was quite happy about it.

Egryn's brother Einion was right on top of the tallest tree, being a lookout in case any big birds came near, when he shouted down, "A chug chug is coming!"

That's a moving arog machine, much bigger than a zoom zoom but slower. Hardly anybody had ever seen one but had heard all about them from some of the elders, especially Selwyn the wanderer.

Everyone had to pick everything up, tables, baskets and tents, and scurry for the trees, bushes or ferns. This hardly ever happened as the lane was not suitable during bad weather and was also a bit overgrown. It couldn't have come at a worse time. Calls of, "Quick, everyone, get under cover!" caused absolute chaos.

The chug chug came right up to the edge of the woods and stopped, and two arogs got out. Everyone peeped through gaps in their cover amongst the leaves, and held their breath. Selwyn the spy was often sent out of the woods to bring back news of the outside world, and he is brilliant at sneaking up to arogs and listening to them speaking. Over the years he has picked up some of the language and can understand mostly what they say. He's got lots of different suits of clothes and looking at the shade of the colour of the grass he sneaked back to his tree, and picked a suit exactly the same shade as the grass by the chug chug as an extra precaution. Everyone else was hiding in the trees, still peeping through the leaves, and they could see Selwyn creeping right up to the chug chug and hiding behind a wheel. They all held their breath, with eyes bulging; you could hear a pin drop.

"Flipping heck, there's a strong smell here, bit like rotten acorns," remarked the taller arog.

"Make sure all the stone ovens behind those trees are turned over so the hot stones are not smouldering, and put lids on the barrels of acorn beer," whispered Brenig the king to the two nearest elves. "The acorn pies can be cooked after they are gone. Be careful and if an arog comes towards you, just forget what you are doing and get aloft."

They were not really ovens, just a hot spot in the sun where they placed food between two stones. Elves were scared of fire.

Everyone watched as the two arogs then got out some metal stands and one kept walking until he was about 20 metres away, holding up another metal stand, while the other looked through one stand, and said things like, "Bit to the left, bit to the right. Up a degree, back two degrees."

Everyone wondered what on earth they were doing.

They did this for two hours.

Nobody dared to move.

Egryn was starving so he moved carefully further back into the tree, sneaked his hand in the nearest basket and pulled a tart out, bit into it and whispered to Iori Llew, "Yummy, rhubarb."

Iori quickly replied, "Pass one to me."

All the others by him told him to pass them out to them as well. It was scary but exciting at the same time. Most had never seen an arog. Some commented that they were a bit smelly and wore funny clothes. Some young elves asked if they were giants.

Selwyn could see them sitting in the chug chug and eating, so he took the risk of sneaking back from the branch to the nearest trunk and gingerly got down onto the floor.

Egryn dropped a tart down to him which he gobbled in one bite and sneaked back to a little bush, right by one of the arog's legs as he had come out of the chug chug saying it was too stuffy inside.

Suddenly one of the arogs shouted out, "OK, it's time to collect everything up."

"Well, that's the first plot marked out, as only one's been sold so far, we can do the other two when they are sold."

They then loaded up the chug chug and Selwyn moved behind a trunk not to get run down and off they went.

After two minutes Einion the lookout, who was still up at the top of the trees, shouted down to Brenig, the king, "They've gone and it's all clear. You can all come out now!"

Brenig ordered (well asked, as elf kings can only suggest) everyone to get on with preparations for the feast, while he had a chat with Selwyn.

Selwyn had a face like a summons. "I've seen arogs do this before, they do it when they plan to build their house. They are marking out where it is going to be."

He had to explain what a house was and what it was made of, etc.

After hearing this, Brenig pondered to think and remarked, "This could be bad news for us all, now I don't want everyone to get scared, so, Selwyn, keep it a secret. We will still have our big party tomorrow, then have a meeting the next day."

Selwyn knew that no elf settlement had ever survived living close to an arog house, but Brenig told him to put a brave face on and not to scare the young ones especially.

"It might not happen. Perhaps they won't come back. We will see what happens tomorrow. This is our most important day of the year so let's get some sleep and get up early as we've got lots to do."

"Just in case, I think we had better have extra lookouts tomorrow," advised Selwyn and Brenig agreed it was a good idea, but hoped they wouldn't be back.

Selwyn wasn't so sure and knew the arogs had come here for a reason, and would definitely be back. Hoping it wasn't going to be the next day, he made his way slowly back to his tree along the branches and hardly slept all night.

CHAPTER THREE

THE BIG PARTY

Elves get out of a trance the minute the sun comes up, and everyone that morning ate a quick breakfast and got on with setting up the tables and finishing preparing the food. A lookout was posted as usual, plus an extra one.

It was a sunny morning and everything was set up in the clearing in front of the biggest oak tree. In the middle of the huge table, which had been erected by joining six other tables, was a huge cake with everyone's name on, as it was everyone's birthday, except for Goronwy who had a separate cake with 222 candles. His was a raspberry cake, his favourite.

While everyone was busy Egryn turned the tap on one of the acorn beer barrels, filled a wooden mug, and gulped it down before anyone could see him, as anyone under 40 was not allowed to drink it.

But he was seen by Brenig who told him, "I can see you, you little rascal, it's OK this year as from now you can drink, but be careful – it's strong and you are not used to it."

On hearing that, he gulped more down. The main feast was due to start dead on midday and with minutes to spare, everything was set up including the big table, and they all took their seats.

Brenig stood up and announced, "Happy birthday to everyone!" and they all chanted it again together.

For the next ten minutes nobody spoke. There was complete silence as they were all stuffing their mouths, except Einion and Trefor, who were still on guard duty on top of the tree.

The only other creatures present were a pair of red squirrels, who have always been friendly with elves and can understand each other, and another table with scraps on for the robins who never used it, as they preferred to land on an elf's shoulder and eat out of an elf's hand.

Seymour the squirrel was full up, so he volunteered to go up the tree and be the lookout so Einion could come down.

"That's very good of you Seymour," he remarked. "I'll do you a favour one day, I won't be long. Then Trefor can come down."

The elves had a special birthday song and when someone was 40 that day, they would have to sing an extra verse at the end, which they must have made up. When everyone was full Brenig announced, "The birthday song!" and they all started singing while Egryn had to stand on the table ready to sing the last verse.

When the song was finished, Egryn jumped off and Goronwy was helped up onto the table and told to read out his leaving poem. When he finished they all gave him three cheers, and he stated, "When you wake up I will be gone, and any of my possessions left, anyone can have. In case I don't have a chance to speak to you in person, all the best and see you in a year's time."

Suddenly Trefor shouted a warning, Seymour came scurrying down the tree trunk and gasped out, "A chug chug is coming, you haven't got much time!"

Everything had to be picked up and lifted into the branches or hidden in bushes, as they didn't have time to put them back in the tree trunks. They couldn't dismantle the big table in time so just covered it with ferns. They had only seconds to spare.

The chug chug pulled up, the only man in it got out and went to the back and lifted out a wooden sign, then bashed it upright into the ground. After studying it for a while, he got back in and drove away. Lucky he did – the big table was now in sight, as some ferns had blown off.

The minute he got out of sight, Selwyn the spy jumped down and looked at the sign. He was the only one who could read. It said "FOR SALE", but he couldn't understand it, so he turned around to check the other side and saw it was in another language which he could understand. This one said "AR WERTH".

He immediately went back to the tree to report to Brenig. Speaking in elfish, he stated that the sign said there were three detached houses being built and two were still available. He had to explain what detached meant.

Brenig said he didn't understand what was going to happen. Selwyn said that he'd seen this thing happen to the elves in *Y Duallt*, which used to be their neighbours' settlement. Arogs came and built new homes and all the elves had to move away and find a new place, even though they've been living in the same spot for hundreds of years. They've never seen any of them since they've moved. This has happened to a lot of other settlements as well.

Lots of the others were listening to the conversation.

Most of the elves said that it wouldn't happen, it was just a piece of wood in the ground, the arogs would forget and never come back. "Let's carry on, it's the best day of the year, now that the feast is nearly over we've got lots to do."

"Yes, I think that's the best idea, carry on as usual. Trefor and Einion, get back up and keep your eyes skinned. Come on everyone, we've got to forget it's happened!"

Everyone's eyes changed colour back to yellow (except Selwyn's) and the special day continued.

Only one birthing bowl was due to be unveiled that day and they all sang the birthing song. Brenig's partner Bronwen brought it out and gave it to Maelgwyn and Ceridwen, and as tradition said it was the female elf, the elfine, who peeled off the silken spider's web cover and announced to the world, "It's a girl and will be called Carys." Everyone cheered. Remember, the names must start with the same letter as the mother and the name must be selected from a special list, as each letter of the alphabet has seven elf and seven elfine names, and only these names can be used.

Next was the carrying of any elf who was 40 to his new tree. As it was only Egryn, he was carried up on the shoulders of his father and his uncle to his tree, and standing on their shoulders he grabbed a branch and swung up. He found the secret entrance and looked in and saw that everything was set up with his new bed, table and chair, etc., and on the table was Goronwy's old walking stick with the names of all the old owners carved on it, including his. He had always wanted that walking stick, so his father decided to pass it on to him.

"The presents next!" someone announced.

So they all went racing over to an old beech tree and saw a pile of presents, each with a name tag on it. Egryn ripped his cover off and to his great joy announced, "A new catapult. Just what I wanted!"

He picked up a bit of an acorn off the floor put it in the catapult, pulled it back and shot it across the clearing, and hit his brother's bum as he was going along on his new wooden scooter. He hid it behind his back but Ednyfed knew it was him as he could tell by his eyes, which were bright yellow as he was so happy. He had to race away while his brother chased him on his scooter, dodging between the trees.

He was lucky as someone shouted, "To the circle!" and they all darted to the special spot in the clearing in the middle of the woods and started to dance and sing.

This went on for hours, as elves know hundreds of songs and about fifty different dances. Everyone forgot about the chug chug except Selwyn, who knew that this was the saddest day ever in the history of their clan of elves. Two lookouts were now to be on guard at all times.

At exactly midnight the party ended, and everyone went to their own tree after clearing everything away. It was common for a few elves to fall out of the trees as they had drunk too much acorn beer, but remember an elf can fall and still land perfectly on their feet, so nobody was really hurt.

Egryn found it really strange, sleeping on his own in his own tree. He was used to his brother Ednyfed snoring and he knew every creaking noise of the branches, and swishing of the leaves. His tree was on the edge of the wood, so the wind was stronger and the noises louder and he couldn't sleep for ages.

He wanted to be fresh in the morning because as he was now an adult, he could vote for the king or queen to carry on for another year, and could take part in the annual ball game. Also there might be a partnership.

If an elf wanted to go into this partnership, arogs call them weddings, then on the night of March the 1st the elfine sneaks in, and puts a honeysuckle mark on their forehead while they are sleeping. Every elf has its own shaped mark, and when the elves wake up and feel the mark they can tell by touching around its shape, then they have to get their family's love spoon. They then must give it to a pair of robins who fly with it, and deliver it to the female.

It didn't happen every year.

CHAPTER FOUR

NEW PARTNERS

On March the 2nd, everyone had breakfast together – well, I call it breakfast but remember elves are so small, light and thin they don't eat much, and as they had a feast the day before some were not hungry. Egryn certainly wasn't as he had a bad head from the acorn beer, which he was not used to.

He was still lying in his bed feeling terrible, when his brother Einion came rushing in. "Quick, get up, *brawd* [brother], you will never guess what's happened!"

"Oh, I feel rotten, my head hurts," mumbled Egryn.

"Serves you right, I told you not to drink too much. Quick, quick, Ednyfed has a honeysuckle mark on his forehead. Come and see!"

They dashed to the breakfast table in the clearing, nearly everyone else was there. The families usually sat together and they asked Ednyfed if he had sent the spoon. He said he had, and they wanted to know who it was, but he wasn't allowed to say.

"Come on, tell us, we are dying to know who it is!"

"No, I can't! Just get on with your food as the election will take place soon."

Shortly after everyone had eaten, Brenig stood up and announced, "The vote for leader will now take place."

Everyone stopped eating and listened while Brenig explained that he would like to carry on if they wanted him.

An old elf named Taliesin stood up; he was the best storyteller of all and knew hundreds of tales from the past. He exclaimed, "I believe that now is not the time to change leaders, as we don't know what the arogs are going to do. The sign means trouble we've never had before. We could be entering the worst time in our history."

Everyone's eyes got darker and darker, perhaps the darkest they'd ever been. Taliesin was considered to be the wisest of the wise.

"Whoever wants Brenig to stay on should stand up now," he declared.

Instantly, everyone stood up.

"An excellent decision, now will everyone please sit down!"

Brenig now stood up. "I thank you from the bottom of my heart. I truly felt that I had come to the end of my time as king and I do believe that it's about time we had an elfine in charge, as the last three have been male elves. I was going to stand down, but because of the crisis I think it's best if I carry on and I can see you all think the same. So once I again I thank you and look forward to being king again this year and to next year when I hope that we all vote for an elfine to take over. I am honoured to lead you again this year and hope that we are able to continue to live as we have done for thousands of years."

After he sat down they all stood up and sang the leader's welcoming song, which was the seventh time Brenig had heard it.

They sang it quite sadly.

"Now everyone pay attention for that's enough gloom for the day, because we have a partnership! Will the elf who had a mark on his head please stand up!"

To everyone's surprise two did, Ednyfed and Maelgwyn. Nobody could remember when this last happened, as it hadn't for ages. They had to stand on the table so everyone could see them. It was so exciting. All the elves, especially the elfines, waited for the signal for the females to be revealed.

Bronwen, the queen, waited for ages then signalled for the partnership tunes to be played on an instrument that looked like a modern harp, except it was made of wood. When the tune changed, Bronwen signalled for the two elfines to stand up and they danced seven times around the table. Egryn looked at them and wondered which one was going to be his sister-in-law. The two girls were Aneira and Dwynwen. They were both beautiful.

Nobody knew which one was going to go to which one. Elves gossiped, saying they thought Aneira was going to go to Maelgwyn, others disagreed, and as soon as the seven laps were completed the music stopped. There was complete silence and the two elfines slowly moved towards their new partners. It seemed to take ages, everyone held their breath and the two elves got up on the table one at each end. The two females stood watching and ever so slowly, each one turned to face their new partner.

A special tune started, the males walked to their new partners and kissed them on their foreheads. The elfine then brought out the small love spoon and gave it to the elf. When he accepted it back, the partnership was sealed and everyone stood up and sang the partnership song while the two couples gracefully waltzed around the table. When the song ended, the dance stopped, the elves stepped down and the elfines were picked up off the table and carried over to their new seats by their new families.

Sometimes years went by when there were no partnerships, so having two on the same day was so memorable.

CHAPTER FIVE

THE BIG MATCH

Next was the big match. Everyone walked to the clearing on the edge of the wood. At each end was a really big oak tree. The winning team had to touch their opponents' tree with a wooden ball made out of oak. If you were touched you had to pass the ball, and if it touched the ground, it was given to the other team. It was seven-a-side, one team was all elves and the other all elfines.

Elves are very light on their feet and are brilliant at dodging and side-stepping. Taliesin had the big oak shield ready to give to the winning captain. Records are kept, and he stated that the record showed that elves had won 1274 times and the elfines 1283 times. Last year the elves won, so the elfines were determined to win back the cup. Egryn was not picked this year because they guessed he would have a bad head, as they knew it was the first time he had drunk acorn beer.

It was a really exciting game that year and really fast. Egryn was running out of breath just watching and thought the game had gone on for hours, but it was only 45 minutes.

The first team to score seven times wins, and the elfines did it again.

The rest of the day everyone sat down and listened to the music played by the harp and the wonderful tunes played by the reed flutes. There were two more big days to come before the yearly festival ended.

In the morning they had a competition a bit like modern golf. Only they used a stick to hit an acorn at a mushroom. There were seven different mushrooms to aim for. All ages could have a go. There was an under 40 competition and another one for over 40s.

The rest of the day was filled by story and poetry readings so everyone would have a rest. The big table, which could be folded up into sections and hidden inside the big oak, was set up. Everyone sat around in order of age, not in families. Anyone under ten had to sit on a branch of a tree to listen, then one by one starting with the youngest, they had to stand up and recite a verse they made up. It had to have at least four lines and not more than twelve.

Bronwen the queen decided the winner, who received a bowl of spiced honey as a prize. She was the only one not allowed to enter.

While all this was going on, two elves were always positioned at the top of the trees as lookouts, but so far the arogs hadn't returned to interrupt the festival.

In the two weeks before, you could enter a story competition and the best three, picked by the queen again, were announced. They had to each in turn read out their story aloud. It had to be less than ten minutes and this time the king picked the winner and awarded him, or her, a wooden sundial.

To finish the day in the evening a fashion show took place. All the clothes the elves wore were made out of natural materials from the forest: grass, reeds, rushes, big leaves, petals, etc., and most of the clothes were waterproof. Again they sat around the table and the contestants paraded down the table wearing the costume they had designed. They had to parade twice, once when it was cloudy and once when the sun was out. Rhiannon had won it ten years running.

"I'm not entering this year as I want someone else to have a chance!" she declared, and everyone cheered.

"Well done!" replied the queen. "A good idea."

Different flowers were in fashion every year – this year it was tulips. Some brilliant shaped hats were worn, and it was very difficult to pick a winner. Every year the winner of this competition was picked by a red squirrel, so Seymour was there from the beginning, watching high up from a branch overlooking the table. It was a good choice as everyone was belonging and everyone was a cousin to everyone, so they had to have a judge who didn't have any relatives.

The red squirrels had lived in this wood as long as the elves and it was the only wood for miles around which hadn't got grey squirrels. They tried to come into the woods many times but the elves, who can sneak up to anyone, would pinch their bottoms, and when they turned around no one was there. This happened every time and in the end they gave up, said there must be ghosts in the wood and left. Every year the red squirrels handed over half of a huge pile of nuts they'd gathered as a thank you to the elves, and the elves helped them by getting the nuts and berries from the thin branches that the squirrels can't get to.

Seymour and his partner Edwina decided that this year's winner was Bedwyr as they especially liked his tulip-shaped footwear. The day ended and they all had an early night, as tomorrow was the last day when all the sporting competitions were taking place. But before the night ended, Egryn and his best friend Iorwerth (who everyone called Iori Llew, except Goronwy who always called him Mr Llywelyn), and the squirrels, went to the signpost, wrapped a rope made out of rushes around it, heaved and pulled the sign down and dragged it to the pond.

Egryn declared, "This sign is not going to spoil tomorrow. If they can't see it, they won't worry about it. Now let's get some sleep, I can't wait until tomorrow."

CHAPTER SIX

THE RACES

Again everyone was up early as there were a lot of races and competitions to get through. Idris the weather expert studied the sky, breathed in the air and stated, "It will start to rain at mid afternoon so we had better get started straight away."

The races were in age categories: 0–5, 5–10, 20–40, 40–100 and over 100.

The young events started first. They had sprints, walking on hands, wheelbarrow with partner, long jump, skipping and balancing an acorn on your head, rolling acorns up the hill races. The older ones played rolling acorns slowly towards a mushroom, very much like modern bowls. There were lots of scooter races around the wood. The older ones had extra events: catapult target shooting, archery, three-legged races with a partner and a hurdles race. After a quick lunch before the rain came they moved to the lily pond, and this time they had to run over it, stepping on lilies to get to the other side and back. Elves eat very little and are very light, so can walk on the top of water on leaves.

Alis Hâf was so light on her feet that they said she could run over a spider's web.

"Come on, you lot, I bet you all my acorns, I will win again!"

"No chance," replied Iori Llew. That was a good decision as she won easily.

Just before the rain came was the last event. Only over 40s could enter, so Egryn was in it for the first time. You had to get a leaf off a tree and climb to the top of a certain oak tree, and go on a certain spot on a certain branch. Then you sat on the leaf, pushed off and paraglided in the air and the one who landed the furthest away won. You had to judge the wind just right. Too weak and you went straight down and too strong you went upside-down. A number of elves had to go high up in different trees as extra lookouts with catapults, just in case the buzzards came. They scanned the skies, while the other two who were still up there kept a look out for the arogs.

Egryn was nervous as paragliding for elves under forty years old was banned, but if older you would have been practising for weeks. His best friend Iori Llew was a year older so was more experienced. Egryn was the first to go, launched himself too early, flew five metres, turned upside-down and landed on his head.

Iori was laughing so much he nearly missed his turn, as you had one minute to sit on the launching pad. But he pushed off just in time and managed to go about 20 metres. The winner was Eluned, she was light even for an elf, managed to stay in the air for two minutes and glided around in circles. Everyone reckoned she was the best ever. You were not allowed to join leaves together for this competition.

I expect you are wondering how Egryn's best friend has a different name, two in fact – well, he hasn't. There are only certain names you can pick, each letter had seven elf names and seven elfine names. Remember you had to have a name beginning with the same letter as your mother, so sometimes you had to have the same name as someone else. So say the first one was called Iorwerth, the second Iorwerth was called Iorwerth Llywelyn (shortened to Iori Llew as it's a long name) and the third one, which didn't happen very often, was Iorwerth Rhys (Iori Rhys). For the girls, the first one was say Lowri, then the second one would be Lowri Hâf and the third Lowri Eleri.

As the last elf finished floating and Eluned was awarded a silver cloak spun out of spider's web as the usual prize, it started to rain just as Idris had said.

"C'mon everyone, let's clear up!" suggested Bronwen. So they all dismantled the table and gathered up all the folded benches and bowls and baskets, and headed for cover inside their trees. If it was light rain they could find a spot covered by leaves, but otherwise they had to go in. All the trees had secret entrances that nobody other than an elf would notice.

Iori Llew went with Egryn to his new tree, as he was going to rub some special ointment that he got off Alis Hâf on his head, which was still hurting, and to tease him about his terrible flight.

He started to rub it in and Egryn shouted, "Awch, that stings!"

"Don't be such a baby, it only takes a few seconds to work." And it did.

"Now let's play this new game I've made, it's a gift for your new house."

In winter months elves played dice games a lot as it passed the time, especially if the weather was bad and they were stuck inside the tree trunks.

Riddle guessing games were also popular. It rained for the rest of the day, Iori Llew stayed the night, and they stayed up late playing on flutes, singing songs and playing the riddle game which Iori Llew was very good at, whilst listening to the rain playing a tune on the tree trunk.

Iori Llew had one go left, thought for ages and finally said, "What's got a flat bottom, one wheel, two legs and flies?"

Egryn couldn't get it, and said, "I give up, what is it?"

"My father's wheelbarrow full of squirrels' poo."

They both laughed at the answer.

Just before they went to sleep, Selwyn the squirrel popped in and gave him a special housewarming gift. He had retrieved part of the sign, and chewed around it to get a large letter "E" on its own. He then used special glue from certain plants and stuck it on to a piece of wood so Egryn could display it on the wall.

"It's a letter which starts your name, called E."

Elves never wrote, there was not much need, they had great memories and could remember hundreds of stories and songs. Very little was ever written down.

"Thank you, I will stick it on the wall in the morning,"

Egryn said, and Seymour made his way back to his own tree after having an acorn supper. It was a sandwich made up of a few acorns coated in syrup, wrapped up in a hawthorn tree leaf.

CHAPTER SEVEN

THE DIGGER

When you get to 40, you must learn skills off the older elves. You would spend four weeks learning off different ones. Today Egryn was going to start his month being trained by Wmffre, who made ropes out of branches, twigs, rushes and leaves. He was in charge of repairing and storing the very, very, very long rope they used to reach the farmer's field about a mile away. Elves don't eat other animals so they need lots of fruit and vegetables.

When the farmer's crops are fully grown, during a dark, moonless night they stretch the rope all the way to his field. Every 20 metres or so they slip it over a Y-shaped stick. On the rope are little baskets and they pull out a vegetable, say a small carrot, or potato, etc. and place it in the basket. The rope goes in two directions and in their clearing they have got a big wheel connected to a pulley system which moves the rope in a circle, so all the vegetables move slowly towards their woods.

Some elves are in the farmer's field pulling out the vegetables, some placing them in the baskets, some along the way checking the sticks are not falling down, some the other end taking out the vegetables before it turns back, and taking them to be stored inside tree trunks. Seymour is the storing expert, and he stacks those carrots inside the beech tree next to Maldwyn's tree, and so on.

Iori Llew said, "Egryn, you would like Wmffre as he tells great jokes and you will have to go outside the wood with him a lot to search for good materials for the rope. He's got an exciting life. This year I'm learning from Macsen how to join leaves together for larger elves to fly in the sky. I will be able to have lots of goes and I bet I will win the big flying prize one year."

"You can keep it," replied Egryn, "you won't catch me up in one of those. Too dangerous."

Elves are up early at first light. They have no clocks, time is measured by the height of the sun. For the first few hours Wmffre had Egryn feeling different rushes to see how each one had a different texture. Then just as he was showing him certain knots to join things, Selwyn came rushing down from a tree shouting, "CHUG CHUG!" There was a terrible panic and about a minute later a really big chug chug pulled up and two arogs got out.

On of them scratched his bum and, looking puzzled, blurted out, "I'm sure I put a sign by here."

"Well it's not here now and anyway there should be another one in the back but we'll do that last thing before we go home."

They spent the next half an hour getting things out of their chug chug.

Just then they could hear a noise made by a huge chug

chug getting louder and louder, much more than the other one, and Egryn's eyes nearly popped out of his head when this massive chug chug drove into the clearing with its huge tyres making deep tracks in the grass.

Another arog got out and chattered to the others for a bit, then went behind the giant chug chug and dropped the back down to make a ramp. He then climbed up and got into a yellow machine and drove it down the ramp. Selwyn slowly sneaked nearer as he can understand a few arogs' words and found out it was called a "digger".

For the rest of the day they watched as the digger dug a large rectangular trench right in the middle of their clearing. It was one of the loudest noises they had ever heard. Lots of the elves were so sad they couldn't look, many were crying and some found the noise of the digger so loud they were having a headache, put beeswax in their ears, and went inside the trunk so they couldn't see or hear.

By the end of the day three large rectangles were dug, and the clearing was ruined. The earth from the trenches had been dumped into their pond on top of the lilies, and the pond was no more. A new sign was put up in the front and back, and the digger was driven up the ramp and the arog drove off. Before the other one went they unloaded a funny-looking thing on wheels that had a funny shaped metal thing on top with a hole in it. Selwyn said, "Have a good look, that's called a mixer. I've seen enough, I must report to Brenig." And off he went.

After waiting a while before coming down from the trees, a few brave elves walked around the sight looking and touching the things left behind, while some were so upset they went to bed early crying and couldn't look.

"I wonder what it mixes?" pondered Iori, and Egryn replied, "I hope it's soup! Talking of food, let's go and get some."

The only ones that were happy were the robins, as the earth had been churned up. There were hundreds of fat juicy worms wriggling and exposed on the surface, and they ate until their bellies were so full they looked like balloons. Robins were belching for hours.

Whilst Egryn and Iori ate in his tree, they laughed as they heard the robins' continual belching and they tried to do it themselves. But they weren't so good; in fact, Iori nearly made himself sick trying to do it.

CHAPTER EIGHT

THE SCREAMING TREES

As they were the youngest adult males, Egryn and Iori Llew were sent up to the top of the trees with Selwyn the elf spy to watch out for any visitors. They went to the really small branches at the very top. It was a bit dangerous.

Meanwhile Brenig called a meeting – they had time as elves are up with the sun and don't need much sleep anyway. Brenig declared, "I think it's time we considered the terrible idea of moving."

There were groans from the rest and many shouted out, "No, never!"

Hardly anyone had ever left their woods, only Selwyn had walked on a road and this was the first time many of them had even seen an arog. They only went to the edge of the wood for berries or to get vegetables from the farmer's field.

One of the elves said that the arogs were so smelly that he thought his ears had grown two inches in the night. Brenig reminded everyone that they must not be seen, and especially warned the terrible twins Morgan and Meredydd not to get out of their tree all day. He didn't trust them. Anyway, no decision was made, but everyone was very worried and the meeting was broken up when they heard Iori and Egryn shout out, "They are back!"

This time it was even worse; a huge chug chug much bigger than the one with the digger was trying to drive as close to the clearing as possible. It struggled up the lane. Branches were in the way and it had to stop.

The driver got out and told the other arogs, "I can't get any nearer unless that tree and those others are chopped down. I haven't got all day, you had better clear the way now."

Another arog replied, "OK, I will get out my chainsaw as the cement must be poured in the trenches today, as it is the mixer is too far away." And he unloaded something from his chug chug.

Brenig told everyone in those trees to move as silently as possible back into other trees, and all the elves did so. They all had to put their hands over their ears as a really loud, horrible vibrating noise came from a machine the man had in his hand. They saw him walk over to a beech tree, put the machine next to the trunk, turn it on and sawdust flew through the air. The elves could hear the tree screaming but the arogs couldn't. It was horrible. All the young elves were sent much further back and told not to look. To their horror the tree started to wobble and then came crashing down. They all wanted to scream in terror, but they were warned not to alert the arogs to their presence.

Over the next few hours, four trees were cut down and cut into pieces, then dragged by the digger and hauled away and dumped on the other side of the wood. All the elves were crying and their eyes were as black as anyone had ever seen, before turning red and sore from the tears. It was really rare for an elf to cry and if they ever did, they would collect their tears in a bowl for Alis Hâf, as they could be used by her to heal any cuts in seconds.

Even worse, an arog then piled up some of the branches and prepared a bonfire.

"Oh my goodness," gasped Selwyn, "I think they are going to have a fire!"

For the next few hours he kept piling more on until all the branches were burnt. The screaming of the trees was so bad that most of the elves went to Alis Hâf's tree and queued up while she blocked their ears with beeswax.

Some, however, had to stay to remain close to the fire as embers were blowing into the branches and they used fern brushes to knock them off. Lots of the grass was singed and looked black. The terrible twins climbed down.

"Come on Meredydd, I've got a great idea." Morgan jumped down, rubbed his hands in it and blackened his face. They both did it and then went to the other side of the wood and hid behind a tree trunk. When some of the little ones went past after having their ears waxed, they jumped out and frightened them. Bronwen heard the screams, rushed over and saw what was going on.

"Well I could have guessed it was you two getting up to mischief. I thought Brenig told you to stay on your tree. Now get back up this minute and get that rubbish off your faces, or there's no supper for you!"

They did as they were told, as Meredydd especially loved his grub.

Finally, the giant mixer moved nearer and a funnel-like thing was swung out and what looked like thick porridge was poured in the trench, all around it, until it was full. It only filled in one of the three trenches though, as by now it was late and the mixer was empty. So the arog got in and drove away. Shortly after, so did all the others.

After about five minutes Einion was sent up the top tree to check whether they had gone. He announced that it was all clear.

"I wonder what that stuff is," inquired Iori.

"I think it might be porridge," replied Egryn. "Come on, let's go see!"

They both made their way to the edge of the trench.

"Doesn't smell like porridge to me."

"Yes, smells horrible, try a bit."

Egryn put his hand in, stuck his tongue out and licked a bit.

"*Agh, ych y fi*! It's horrible!" and he spat it out straight away.

Brenig saw all this and suggested, "Everyone must be very careful, get some rest and put beeswax in their nose, otherwise you won't sleep because of the strange smell. We will see what happens tomorrow and if they come back, which seems probable, we will have to have a meeting at the end of the day. Things can't go on like this."

They all dispersed and went off to their trees, but sleep was hard to come by.

CHAPTER NINE

A JOURNEY

Egryn woke and wondered what was in his ears and nose. He remembered about the wax, removed it, and realized the smell from the porridge wasn't so bad. It was early so obviously the arogs hadn't arrived. He scampered over the branches and went to wake Iori Llew.

"Come on, lazy bones, wake up." He never moved as the wax stopped him hearing anything. Egryn realized this, so shook him.

"What's happening?" grumbled Iori. "What have you woken me up for?"

"The horrible porridge, remember, let's be the first ones to go and see what's happened to it as it's not smelling any more."

"Have the arogs come yet?"

"No, come on, hurry up, let's get there before Morgan and Meredydd."

They dashed down and approached the trench carefully as they could see it was now a different colour. Egryn leaned over, stretched out his hand and very gingerly poked it.

"Ouch!"

"What's the matter?"

"It's rock hard."

"You are joking."

"No I'm not. Watch me!"

Iori then put both his hands in and to his surprise it was hard all over.

"Watch this!" shouted Egryn, and he jumped in and never sank down at all, in fact he hurt his feet.

Iori did the same and they both walked all around the trench and found it was completely solid.

They decided to report to Brenig straight away and dashed off to his tree.

After hearing their news, Brenig realized they must have a meeting straight away before the arogs arrived, so he sent the two of them around to wake everyone up.

They all gathered together and Brenig explained about the trench, which had now ruined the clearing.

"It can never be the same again. This proves the arogs are here to stay, so we must move away. I had a long chat with Selwyn last night and he told me this would happen. You don't know that over the years, Selwyn was instructed during his wanderings to find other sites where we could relocate to. He believes there are five possibilities."

Everyone groaned, and some shouted, "NO!"

Others said, "Never!"

Only a few elves had ever been onto the rough track that came to the edge of the wood. Eirianwen, who was the oldest female, said, "As you all know I'm 212 years old and I've never been out of this wood all my life, and never will. I'm not going anywhere!"

Lots said the same.

"Well," Brenig replied, "nobody wants to but they might have to. So I'm asking Selwyn [nobody, not even the king or queen, can order an elf to do anything he doesn't want to do, remember] to go back out into the world and check these sites. Selwyn, will you do that please?"

Selwyn answered, "Yes I will, but it would be a good idea if a younger elf came with me just in case something happened. It can be very dangerous in the outer world. Also, one site is not there any more, it is now destroyed. Our world is getting smaller. Woods have disappeared; elf colonies are much fewer with fewer elves. Some colonies have been wiped out by germs caught off arogs, and the few who survived are living like the wild elves, wandering from place to place with no home. It will be a dangerous journey."

Brenig asked for a volunteer, preferably someone younger than a 100 years old.

Meredydd and Morgan instantly shouted out, "We will go!"

"No chance," replied Selwyn. "I can't think of a worse choice. I'm not taking you two."

Egryn, who had always been a bit adventurous, stuck his hand up and shouted, "What about me?"

Iori Llew shouted out, "If he's going, I am as well!"

They all looked at Selwyn. "Actually three would be better, but I never thought two would volunteer as it's very, very dangerous. There's a great possibility that we won't be back. Think about it."

Brenig now spoke. "Are you really sure, have you really

thought about it? It's not just a fun adventure, it's a risky journey and you probably won't return."

Egryn and Iori Llew looked at each other.

Rhiannon and Alis Hâf mumbled, "Please don't go. We are afraid something terrible might happen to you."

They both hesitated.

"I'm going on my own then," remarked Selwyn.

"No you are not," declared Egryn. "I've made up my mind, I'm coming with you."

"So am I!" stated Iori.

Everyone clapped and they gave three cheers for the three volunteers.

"You need to start straight away," Brenig informed them. "There's no time to waste."

They went to get their travelling clothes, and put on new shoes, and to make sure they had their catapults.

Rhiannon rushed to her tree to get some extra clothes she had made which would make them more difficult to see.

Selwyn checked the wind and said that they were lucky as it was blowing in the exact direction towards the first site.

"Macsen, have you made a leaf glider that can carry the three of us?" he asked.

He replied, "I have made one that can carry four, I think, but it has never been tested as it has only just been made. A bit risky. But it should be fine for three."

Selwyn answered, "No time for testing, you two grab your clothes and get on that tree there."

After giving their family cwtches (hugs) they started to climb the tallest tree in the wood. Wmffre took a gang with him and with one of his ropes, they managed to get the big glider up to the top. The three got up and Selwyn unfolded a sail made out of woven ferns.

"Be really careful, boys, when you get on we must keep a balance, so I will be in the middle working the sail. Iori Llew in the back, and Egryn in the front. Remember not to wriggle or move sideways, for if you do I won't be able to keep the balance and we will crash," he explained.

He hoisted the sail up and very carefully they got on. "Whatever you do don't look down," and the other two sat like statues, hardly daring to breathe. Lots of little heads were gazing up at them, except for Alis Hâf and Rhiannon who said that they couldn't look.

Selwyn shouted, "Off we go!" and the others prepared to launch them off the top of the tree.

Some elves lined the branches and watched, expecting them to crash straight down.

Four others had climbed up, the branch was wobbling a bit, and they pushed them off. At first it edged forward, then started to drop, and it looked as if they were going to crash, but a gust of wind got trapped in the sail and they slowly glided up and headed off in the right direction.

The elves on the ground cheered. Alis Hâf and Rhiannon removed their hands and shouted out, "Be careful!"

"Don't take risks!"

"Listen to Selwyn!"

"Please come back!"

As they slowly got smaller and smaller in the distance, the elves wondered if they really would ever return, and just stared in complete silence, nobody daring to speak. Just before they disappeared in the far distance, a chug chug could be heard coming and they all scattered, forgetting about their friends as they were too busy clamouring for safety.

CHAPTER TEN

THE BUILDING BEGINS

This time the usual chug chug came and another bigger one, filled with hundreds of red bits of stone. What were they? They watched as the small red cuboids were unloaded and stacked in a pile. Then some bags were lifted off, cut open, and what looked like porridge was poured in the round machine. This was now filled with water and plugged in. It started to turn around and around and made a terrible noise. They could hear the water sloshing around.

This went on all day and this porridge after a short while was taken out, put on the little red stones and placed in the trench in order in a straight line. They kept repeating this.

By the end of the day a wall of red cuboids one metre high went right around the trench, except for a little gap in the front and back. They were so mesmerized by watching this that they forgot about their friends who had gone off.

That night a few elves, including the terrible twins, went down and touched the cuboids and they didn't move. So Brenig sent down a few of the older ones, and they pushed and heaved but only managed to push down a couple from the top. The ones lower down had gone hard already. Their clearing was ruined. All those games, parties, etc. that had been held in their beloved clearing for hundreds of years probably would never happen again.

To many elves, this clearing was the most important and sacred place in the world. Everyone was so sad they couldn't eat, and their eyes got darker and darker. One of the trees knocked down was an oak, so one family had to go and move into Egryn's tree. They were so upset, their family had lived in that tree for hundreds of years – they knew its smell, every branch, every leaf. The oldest one, Cadwaladr, was nowhere near 222 but still said that in the morning he was going to follow Goronwy.

"I'm off in the morning, I don't want to live in this world any more."

This was the saddest night ever in the history of this group of elves and was forever after called "The Night of the Wall".

Next morning nobody wanted to get up, they all stayed where they were enjoying the quiet, with just the familiar rustling of the branches in their tree. One family cried as they listened to a different noise, as their family tree was gone forever.

Egryn's brothers and Iori Llew's brother took turns to go on watch to check whether the three could be seen coming back, but Brenig said it was too early as they probably wouldn't get the wind in the right direction to fly back. Also Selwyn said they would probably be away for at least five days, might be longer. They missed them so much they still went on watch.

They watched as Cadwaladr trudged off away from the woods with his belongings wrapped in a bag made by Rhiannon, dangling from a stick which he rested over his shoulders.

"Please Cadwaladr, don't go!" pleaded his family, but he replied, "It's no good, I can't stay here." They watched as he disappeared into the distance.

The next day was the worst ever, if that was possible, as the arogs saw a bit of the brick wall had been pushed down. So one drove off and came back with the biggest and nastiest dog they had ever seen. It was a breed the elves had never seen before, and the little elves were reminded not to leave the tree, and not to ever go on the ground.

The dog was chained to a pole and he was able to walk about ten metres in any direction. That day the wall got higher again, they watched in horror as the dog was fed a big lump of meat, and they could see his massive teeth as he chewed it. The little elves were petrified of this monster, and they all moved to the tree furthest away from him.

When the arogs went away for the night they extended the chain, so that the dog could go 20 metres in every direction. None of the elves went down to the ground that night, not even the terrible twins, and they all had to eat whatever berries or food they had stored. That was OK, as elves can survive on very little food.

There's nothing an elf likes more than mischief and very early that morning Meredydd woke Morgan up. It was getting light and the terrible twins made their way to the branch nearest the dog.

"First one to hit him is the winner," whispered Meredydd.

Morgan shot first, rushed it and missed, so Meredydd took his time and copped him on his head.

The dog instantly jumped and barked and tried to run off in the direction he thought the shot had come from, but the chain just about held. They both shot a few more times and hit him again. The dog got madder and madder.

"I've got an even better idea," said Meredydd. "You stay here and keep shooting at him, while I make my way across the branches and shoot at him from the other side."

Meredydd moved around to the tree at the other end and found a spot so they could both fire at the dog from both directions. They shot at his bum, and when he turned and barked the other one would shoot from the other side, and hit his bum again. They did this a few dozen times and the dog was exhausted jumping up and straining, trying to break free from the chain.

When the dog finally collapsed exhausted and fell asleep, the terrible twins stopped shooting, climbed down and went to the wall now that it was safe. However, they found it was now solid and they couldn't move a brick, no matter how hard they pushed.

Someone heard the noise, then went to wake Brenig and told him about them. He left his tree and went to see for himself.

Brenig could see the dog was exhausted and wouldn't be able to break free, so he suggested to the ones who had woken up that now would be a good time to scramble down and get some food from wherever they could find it, and for them to stretch their legs.

The terrible twins thought Brenig would be pleased, but he wasn't. They were taking too many risks and no animal, even if it was a dog, should be harmed, so they were asked not to shoot at it again.

He wasn't sure if they would listen, as they rarely did.

CHAPTER ELEVEN

NO NEWS

When the arogs came in the morning they were happy this time to see no bricks had been pushed down, so they started the generator and got on with the bricking straight away. They also plugged in a machine the elves had never seen before which played very loud music.

They had to cover their ears as it was so loud and harsh – they were used to pipes, flutes and harps playing soothing music, not this banging and shouting. This music was left on all day and most of the elves had a headache and cwtched down inside the trunks of the trees furthest away, even if they weren't oaks. Between the noise and the smells and the dog, the day seemed very long. It seemed as if they were in a nightmare.

The next few days the wall got higher and higher, and they couldn't go down. Brenig had found out that the terrible twins had shot at the dog again, both had their catapults taken off them for two weeks, and were banned from making new ones. Once again they had to go to the squirrel's tree.

Elves are not allowed to hurt and certainly not kill anything. They won't go fishing as it's too cruel. Catapults are only used to knock berries and fruit off high trees to save climbing up, not to cause pain. Also if you recall they can shoot at birds of prey, like buzzards, red kites, kestrels, etc. but that was to frighten them away, not kill them. No elf knew how to fight as they never had to, and any disputes were decided by the king or queen, but that hardly ever happened. They had never heard of the word war.

In the afternoon another big chug chug arrived, a different one.

The new chug chug parked, and large rectangles were very carefully lifted from the chug chug, four of them were fitted around the bottom part of the wall, and four were fitted higher up. What were they? There didn't seem to be anything inside them as you could see through them.

The terrible twins were bored stiff, stuck in all day. That night they pretended to go to sleep so Seymour thought it was OK for him to pop out for some nuts. After exhausting the dog again by throwing stones, as they had no catapults, they climbed down and went to find out. Meredydd went to one of the frames that was stacked against the wall and tried to put his head through, but it banged against something.

"Ouch, it's hard!" and he put his hand on it and found out that you could push it and it still didn't move, it was firm. What was strange was that you could see through it. They were all the same.

This time they decided not to tell Brenig, hoping he wouldn't find out they had defied their ban.

As they made their way back to the tree, they were confronted by Brenig.

"What do you think you are doing? I thought I told you to stay in your tree. Thought I wouldn't find out, did you?"

"We didn't shoot our catapults!"

"No, you just threw stones, just as bad, now follow me."

He marched them to the squirrel's tree at the far end of the wood.

"Now get up Selwyn's tree. If they move, Seymour, you have my permission to bite their bums. This is your last chance."

Seymour made a noise with his teeth and they both scrambled up the tree like mad. "If you place one foot on the ground it will be my pleasure to bite your juicy bums as I've never tasted an elf. I bet you are really juicy."

The squirrels had different rules to elves, and Seymour really would bite them if they got down. In fact he hoped they would. They never moved.

The next few days went by; the house got taller and taller. A roof was put on, but before the tiles were added the elves, as they were stuck in the trees all day, had races jumping across the wooden beams and back. They've got great balance. Brenig gave permission for the terrible twins to leave the tree and join in for one hour. The dog could see them, but soon gave up barking as he couldn't get near them because of the chain.

Alis Hâf, who was the expert at creating potions, took one to Brenig and said if he sprinkled a few drops over the dog's food, it would make him go to sleep in about ten minutes and he would go into a deep coma for about two hours. Other than that it was harmless. Brenig thanked her and said they would use it when they needed to.

Still no sign of the three returning from their journey. They were all getting a bit worried now. Brenig wanted to do anything to delay the construction of the building, but he was afraid an elf might be seen by an arog or bitten by the dog. At the moment he couldn't think of anything.

Brenig was getting seriously worried as the days went by. The three should have been back by now, but he tried not to show it.

To try and keep their minds off worrying, Bronwen the queen announced that there was to be a competition to see who could design a model of an arog. There were no rules. They could use whatever material they liked and it could be any size.

Rhiannon and Alis Hâf were so worried they said at first they wouldn't take part, but once they saw the others starting theirs they couldn't resist it and got on with their own efforts. This helped to pass the time.

CHAPTER TWELVE

THE JOURNEY ENDS

The next day when the arogs arrived, they unloaded and unwound lots of what they called wires and took them into the house. One of the elves waited until the dog ate his dinner and was dozing, then sneaked down and grabbed a piece of wire which had been cut off a longer piece. He took it straight to Brenig.

He touched it and bent it but didn't have a clue what it was used for. Suddenly a wood pigeon landed on Brenig's tree.

He was gasping for breath but managed to blurt out, "I've seen them."

"Seen who?"

"The three elves."

"Where?"

"Coming from the west."

"How far away?"

"A long way, they probably won't be back until tomorrow."

"That's great news."

Brenig passed out the news. Everyone was so happy and relieved and so glad they were coming back safe.

In the morning an elf was positioned at the very edge of the wood to warn them about the dog, and to show them the best way to avoid him and all the arogs and their chug chugs.

Everyone was up even earlier, if that was possible. They were all really excited and the tops of the trees were crammed with elves, including the terrible twins, whom Brenig had pardoned and allowed to leave Seymour's tree. They were all scanning the horizon for the returning three.

The day went on, the sun got higher, and still no sign. Just as it was getting dark and the arogs had left, the pigeon could be seen hurrying back.

He was completely out of breath – they had never seen him flying so fast.

"I've got terrible, terrible news!"

"What is it, what's happened?" they all asked.

After gasping down a few gulps of air the pigeon managed to say, "Selwyn has been attacked by a buzzard."

Brenig replied, "Is he hurt?"

"Yes, really badly."

"What about the other two?"

"They are not hurt and are trying to stop the blood seeping out of his wound. They sent me here to get help. That's all I know."

"How far away are they?" inquired Brenig.

"Quite a way," the pigeon said, "but if someone can follow me I will show them where they are. It's about two hours' journey on foot. Selwyn is injured too much to move."

Brenig couldn't order anyone to go. But he knew someone had to.

Alis Hâf shouted out, "I will go!"

She was the best in the whole woods at healing cuts and wounds. She knew every herb, and by mixing potions and using her bowl of tears she could heal almost anything. She could put her hand on a leaf, spread a certain potion mixed with tears, hold it on an elf's cut and it would heal in two minutes. However, deep wounds would take much longer. As they had never been to war, had no weapons other than a catapult, never quarrelled, and had no enemies other than certain birds, they hardly ever saw deep wounds. She had never been out of the settlement but Egryn and Iori Llew were her best friends, and Selwyn was her uncle.

"It's very dangerous! Are you sure?"

"Absolutely."

"Well, it is getting dark so you had better go with the pigeon at first light. Let's hope he's still alive in the morning. You will never find him tonight."

Everyone was too worried to sleep and the night was long. Just as Alis Hâf had packed all her healing potions in a leaf bag and was about to start out, a call came from the top of the tree.

"I think they are coming!"

They looked and they could see four elves, not two, one at each corner of a makeshift stretcher, carrying someone who was obviously Selwyn. Einion shouted out that he would show them the way in to avoid the dog.

When they reached the clearing, the stretcher was lifted into Alis Hâf's healing tree, and some of the elves fainted when they saw Selwyn's wounds as most had never seen blood. The youngsters were told not to look and taken to the other parts of the wood.

Before they could ask Egryn and Iori Llew what had happened, Brenig thanked the two wild elves for helping and asked who they were.

They said that they were Iwan and Gruffydd, two brothers. The king asked them how two elf brothers had names beginning with different letters, as this was unheard of. They replied that in their clan, only the girls' names had the same letter as the mother. Strange, thought Brenig.

"How did you find them?" he asked.

They explained that they lived on their own and wandered around the country avoiding arogs, and enjoyed themselves having adventures. Their settlement was destroyed about ten years ago. Their forest has since been destroyed by arogs so they could never go back. Therefore they set up again in three different camps, but they were no use as arogs got nearer and nearer, and eventually they had to split up into small family groups. In the end just their family was left on its own. Arogs were everywhere and a huge road called a motorway was being built, and they were sent out to travel as far as possible to try and find a new site nowhere near any arogs.

They found out they liked exploring and wandering, and only went back every few months. Gradually they stayed away longer and longer, and the last time they went back they found their parents and sister had died, they think from a fever caught off the arogs.

Brenig thanked them for helping and said they could stay as long as they liked. Remember, wild elves are not usually welcomed, but due to their kindness, they were allowed. They looked around and said they wouldn't stay for long as they saw the house, and said that many of the elves they had seen in their travelling were ill, as well as his family dying, after catching germs off arogs. The longer they stayed the more dangerous it was. But it would be nice to stay safely with friends for a while, and they would stay until Selwyn got better or died. The young elves asked what germs were, as elves are never ill.

Alis Hâf then reported, "I think I might be able to heal Selwyn, but his wounds are very deep and he must not move for at least a week. He must stay in my tree for probably much longer. I need a few elves to go outside the settlement to get certain plants I need."

She was not short of volunteers.

Egryn and Iori Llew were exhausted, and now that Alis Hâf said that she could probably heal Selwyn they were relieved and just wanted a good sleep to recover. Before doing that they stated that if it wasn't for Iwan and Gruffydd they would never have got back, they couldn't carry Selwyn on their own as he was too heavy. They could only crawl, and the wind was in the wrong direction to glide. They tried but crashed and ruined the glider. They didn't know how to make a new one properly. Also they had to cross a few big fields, and the buzzard was still circling, looking for them. Iwan and Gruffydd knew all the safe ways to cross fields, it was a bit longer but with four carrying they could go faster.

Einion asked them, "What's happened to your ears?"

They replied, "Nothing. Why? What's the matter with them?"

"They are much bigger than they used to be."

Iwan interrupted and stated that it's a fact that he and Gruffydd had got bigger ears than any other living elf, not counting the wild ones. It was because they had wandered so much, and smelt so many new different aromas. All wild elves ended up with bigger ears. Egryn said that he was too tired to care, and he and Iori Llew both went and laid down and were sleeping deeply after two minutes, and even closed their eyes.

Before he fell into a deep sleep as well, Egryn was asked to give details of what happened. He explained that according to Iori, Selwyn was ahead of them when he was attacked by a buzzard as he didn't know he was near their nest. It was only brilliant shots with his catapult that saved Selwyn's life, as it was just about to fly off with him. When Iori's shots hit its claws, just at the right time, the bird dropped him. They then rushed towards him where he landed and hid him in the ferns. They were hiding and trying to stop the flow of blood when the two wild elves dashed into the same area of ferns and had a shock when they saw them. But lucky for them, they just happened to be passing through and helped immediately to stop the flow of blood.

CHAPTER THIRTEEN

LISTENING TO THE OUTSIDERS

In the morning, Iwan and Gruffydd told Brenig they were going to explore the house before the arogs came, and were not scared by the dog as they had come across many in their travels.

"Are you sure you are not scared to go in? Yesterday the arogs took in some blue, green and red flexible long rope-like things."

Iwan replied, "No, we are not because during our journeys we have come across what the arogs called holiday homes, which are empty most of the year and have stayed in a few. One time the arogs arrived late in the day, and we spent that night in the same house. In fact we stayed a few days watching how the arogs cooked and washed etc. We learnt how the indoor pond which they called a bath worked, and how on hot days they turned a switch and cold air came on, and on cold days hot air came on.

"One day Gruffydd watched an arog open a fridge door, and was getting different items out, so he peeped inside, and as she turned around he jumped in, and hid behind some items. She took one more item out, then closed the door. He was trapped inside and couldn't get the door open. Lucky for him I was watching, and while the arog was making something, I tiptoed up to the fridge and reached up to the bottom of its door and heaved. I couldn't budge it. Gruff was stuck inside and was getting cold. I didn't know but he wrapped himself inside a lettuce to keep warm.

"What could I do? Well, the arog had a little bowl of milk on the worktop, and every now and then would dip a brush in some white liquid and spread it over some pastry. While she went out of the room, I climbed up the leg of a stool and pushed and pushed the bowl. But it was too heavy and I couldn't move it, so I jumped in the bowl and started drinking it. I recognized it as the white stuff I had seen an arog get out of a cow. I drank and drank but it didn't go down much. So I had to keep drinking. My belly was bloated but I kept on. After hearing some water running in the distance, I could hear the arog's footsteps coming nearer, and before the door was opened I jumped out and hid behind the leg of a stool.

"The arog picked up the brush, and when she dipped the brush in she saw there wasn't enough milk, so she went to what she called the fridge to get more. When Gruff heard the door open and a light come on he saw the arog lift up a bottle of the white stuff and when she turned, he jumped out before she came back to put the bottle back and close the door. That was a really close shave. Oh yes, we've had many adventures in their houses. We have got used to being in one at the same time as one of them."

"Have you really? Tell me more," pleaded Brenig.

"Well just one more as we need to explore this one before the arogs come. Gruffydd, you can tell this one."

"OK but remember we only went in one if they didn't have any pet dogs or cats, and only for a few hours, unless it was empty. Well, once an arog family had a huge bird called a parrot in what they called a cage. When one of us went in the room, only the parrot could see us and he would call out 'Who's a good boy then!'

"Like all elves we like mischief, so while the arogs were watching a box with moving pictures and words, which they called a television, we would pop out from behind a piece of furniture, and the parrot would call out. We kept doing it, and the arog children would ask their mam to get the parrot to shut up, so she would put a blanket over his cage so he couldn't see."

They went exploring then. When they came back they informed Brenig that they could both understand some arogs' speech, and even read some words. They then explained to Brenig that the sign said three houses were going to be built, and the trenches were for two more. Also the number three was crossed out and replaced by a two, so that probably meant that one being built was sold. That probably explained why the other two trenches were empty, as they were not sold yet.

Later that day, not long after the arogs arrived, Iwan and Gruffydd watched them and explained to Brenig what they were doing. What the items were going in the house, what the machines were for and so on.

Egryn and Iori Llew woke after their nap, and had to report to the king. They told Brenig that the journey was a waste of time, as they found nowhere where there were enough oak trees together in a safe spot well away from arogs. Remember going up lots of the hills was no good as oaks only grow below a certain height, and so do many berries, plants, herbs and fruit.

Iwan and Gruffydd agreed, and they said there was no point in going to look again in that direction, as they had travelled for a few years now and they didn't know of any suitable places where they could all settle in that direction.

Brenig said, "That's really bad news, not what I was hoping for. I need to think, we must have a full meeting tonight after the arogs have left, and there's no noise. Meanwhile I am going to have a further chat with Iwan and Gruffydd. They must have found some suitable places in the other direction. Now, all of you get an early night and the meeting will commence one hour after first light."

CHAPTER FOURTEEN

THE MEETING

What a day! The meeting was called and Brenig asked Alis Hâf to give them the latest news about Selwyn.

She explained to the whole settlement, pronouncing, "Selwyn has had a good night and the worst is now over. He is not going to die."

They all cheered like mad.

"However, his wounds are deep where the buzzard's claws had gone right in, but I have cleaned them by applying certain poultices every hour all through the night, I am sure that he will make a full recovery. Nevertheless, he cannot be moved at all for at least a week, probably two, and only then on a stretcher. However in about a month he should be able to walk, and another month be back to normal."

Someone shouted out, "Three cheers for Alis Hâf!" and the noise caused some leaves to wobble and drift off the nearest branches.

When the noise died down, Brenig stood up and declared, "We cannot stay here!"

Some groaned, and he went on to say that Iwan and Gruffydd had explained to him some details he wasn't sure about. Three houses were being built, not just the one that had been started, so the clearing would be completely gone and the pond also.

This caused great consternation and everyone started talking to each other. Brenig asked Iwan and Gruffydd if there was anything else they needed to know. They both stood up and explained that there was a good chance that being so close to an arog, they could catch certain germs. These germs would make them ill. They could die. This had happened to their own family. This caused more groans.

No one wants to leave their ancestral home; for many it would be the first time.

"Time to take a vote," announced Brenig, "all those who think we should leave the settlement please stand up."

Nobody moved at first, but then one or two stood up, then a few more and eventually almost all of them did.

"Well, now that we have decided a move must take place, I've got some more information for you. There is nowhere near here where we all can stay together. But only half a mile away there is a little grove of trees with just four oaks. Perhaps three families could go there, with mine. According to Iwan and Gruffydd there's two other groves about a mile further away. One has three trees and another has two. It will be a squash, and we will not all be together. Also some trees would have to have more than one family in them, but if we planted more, eventually our long-term aim is to have everyone together again.

"Someone will have to stay here, as we don't want other animals moving in to our sacred trees, especially the woodpeckers, and we need to stop the grey squirrels coming in and settling, because the red ones are staying. They have decided not to move. The fruit trees and bushes will need looking after as well, and must be picked ready for others to come and collect the fruits. Also we need to realize that it will be impossible to lead our lives with no contact with arogs if we stay here. Wherever we go we won't be far away from arogs, therefore we need to learn about their habits. What do you think?"

Lots of hands shot up, and everyone had a different opinion. The older ones still didn't want to move but Iwan and Gruffydd told them that they had listened to the arogs talking, as they were good at sneaking up, and one said that he wouldn't be surprised if eventually this would be a little village and lots more houses would be built. There was a massive groan when they heard this.

A vote was taken again, and it was decided that they all would move in two weeks' time. Lots were drawn to see who was going where, and it was decided that the nearest one would eventually be developed into the main camp. Brenig asked for a volunteer to stay, perhaps a different one for a month each. Egryn's hand went up first and he was chosen. Iwan and Gruffydd said that they would stay with Egryn for the first week, but then they were off on their travels.

The next morning small groups were sent out to the new sites to get the trees ready to move into. Trunks had to be hollowed out. Also, they were to start planting new trees and setting up a perimeter of brambles around each site. Enough to keep any arogs out if they ever came to these areas. Lots of new bushes would be planted inside the brambles so that they had fruit and berries inside the camp.

They were so busy preparing for the move that they almost forgot the house was nearly finished, and chug chugs kept coming and items were carried into the house.

They had a big shock when the electricity was suddenly connected and lights came on, then off, then on again. Some elves said they didn't know arogs could do magic.

Iwan and Gruffydd said that they had seen it before, and that arogs can switch it on and off whenever they like, all over the house. The little elves asked if you burnt your hand if you touched the light, but it was explained that unless you put your hand on what they called a bulb, you didn't feel a thing.

Also they can make the house hotter, it can be frosty outside but the house can be boiling inside. The elves were amazed and said that really must be magic.

That night Iwan and Gruffydd led a party of four elves including Egryn and Iori Llew up the drainpipe, along the roof and in through a little window, down the stairs and into the lounge. They usually went through the letterbox but the proper door wasn't fixed yet. They were told to settle down on the new carpet and they explored the house and found a switch with numbers on. This might be it, they turned the switch and waited. While they waited, some of the elves had a competition to see who could create the best routine of exercises on the new soft carpet.

Rolling about and somersaulting was warm work, but after a while someone said that it was really hot in there now. They could feel the heat coming from a metal thing on the wall. It was so hot that they completed the gymnastics routines almost naked. Before going back out Gruff turned the switch back off. He knew what to do.

Egryn and Iori Llew became great friends with Iwan and Gruffydd, and they loved to have little wrestling games together on the carpet. They had to do it after the arogs had gone. They would also wrestle on a branch and the winner would be the last one standing on the same one. They didn't get hurt as elves can tumble in the air and land on their feet from great heights.

CHAPTER FIFTEEN

BOAT RACES

Every night for the rest of the week, a party of four elves, Egryn, Iori Llew, Alis Hâf and Rhiannon, would go into the house with the outsiders. All the others were too scared to go in. Brenig said it would be a good idea because they might one day have to come back here and live near a house, if there was nowhere else. There was no guarantee that their new settlements were safe. These four were the most sensible. The terrible twins wanted to go but were told not to, and were still being watched by the squirrels.

Rhiannon loved to rub her hands on what they called the carpets. She found some bits left over from a newly laid one, and had the four of them struggle to carry the smallest bit out towards her tree, where she could use it to make winter hats.

The next night Iwan and Gruffydd (who remember are now called the outsiders) told the four to bring their bathers. They didn't have any, most elves had never swum in their lives, so Rhiannon measured them up and made them some out of a piece cut out from a carpet.

That night the outsiders took them upstairs to a special room which had a massive white tub in. Gruffydd turned a switch on and Iwan put a small round thing in a hole in the bottom of the tub. He then went and tried to turn a metal thing at the top of the tub, explaining that the arogs called it a tap. He couldn't budge it so Gruffydd helped. Still no good. In the end the six of them had to twist it and eventually a small amount of water came out. Iwan explained that if you turned it more then it came out much faster, but would be hard to turn off as it would be too hot and not too safe.

They watched the tub fill up slowly, then Gruffydd jumped in with a little boat he had brought with him made out of reeds. Soon all six were in, all had their own light little boats. They kept away from the tap, which continued to trickle.

They had lots of races but were careful not to fall in, as elves can't swim much, except for the outsiders. After hours of fun they got out and the outsiders grabbed a chain and pulled, and it moved enough for the water to go out and then all six turned the tap back off, being careful not to be burnt by the hot water.

For the next four nights they went to the tub and the outsiders, who could swim a bit, got the four others to try it. When they got in though, their bathers soaked up the water and got too heavy so Rhiannon had to cut and design new ones out of woven grass, which didn't soak up the water.

The terrible twins Morgan and Meredydd wondered where they disappeared to at night, and they sneaked away when the squirrels were not looking, and followed them. They had never been in a house before. The others heard them scrambling up the drainpipe. The arogs had been painting and some white sheets were left behind to stop paint going on the floor. The six of them lifted one up and hid behind the door and put the sheet over their heads. When the twins slowly opened the door and gingerly stepped inside, the six of them jumped out together and made a ghostly noise. You've never seen two elves run so fast. They skidded down the shoot like Billy Whizz, scraped their bums, and ran and hid the other side of the woods back in the squirrel's tree, after nearly running over the dog who was sleeping.

When a new door was put on they could now go through the letterbox, but one early morning before the arogs came and the wet dew was still everywhere, the outsiders carried a pile of ferns and stacked them a few inches from the bottom of the drainpipe. They then climbed up and poked their head above the top of the pipe. The others watched as they got to the top and shouted, "Watch this but keep back!"

Next thing they knew, a few seconds later, Iwan came shooting out of the bottom of the drainpipe at a great speed, flew in the air and landed on the top of the ferns. Gruffydd quickly followed. The others then had a go but were told to start halfway up and if they liked it, to keep going up a bit higher every time. Alis Hâf and Rhiannon were less scared than the boys and were the first to do it from the top. They were told to only do it when it was a bit wet because when they first did it when it was dry and sunny, they would stop halfway down and have sore bums.

The outsiders asked the others if they had ever eaten any arogs' food. They said they hadn't so next day they both sneaked up to the spot where the arogs had their break when it was dry, under a tree and sitting on an old log. They opened their food box and pinched some out. Taking it back to show the others, they asked them to have a nibble. The first had a terrible smell and they each had the smallest nibble possible, then spat it out.

"It's disgusting, the pong is terrible," shouted Rhiannon.

"What is it?" inquired Alis Hâf.

The outsiders laughed and explained it was a fish called a salmon. Elves won't kill so most had never eaten a fish or smelt one before.

The next one had a strong smell, a bit like sweaty feet.

"This is even worse!" exclaimed Iori. "Who can eat anything that smells like this?" "Not on your nelly!" replied Egryn. "Have you got anything that tastes a bit sweeter and doesn't smell like Iori's socks?"

"Try this then. Bet you like it," and Egryn passed over a bit of something which he had broken off a large, round item.

It was dark on one side and Alis Hâf nibbled it first.

"It's absolutely brilliant. Everyone try it, go on."

Egryn broke more bits off and passed them around. There were cries of, "Superb", "Gorgeous", "More please!"

They gobbled lots more and Egryn watched with a smile on his face and when they finished, explained that it was a chocolate biscuit. They demanded another one and they all licked the one side first, and all said it was the nicest thing they had ever tasted. It was actually a Chocolate Hobnob.

They couldn't eat it all as the arog would notice, so they put the food boxes back under the tree with most of the food still there. It was exciting as every day, the outsiders sneaked small amounts and they tasted some food items for the first time ever. One arog had a sweet tooth and they enjoyed eating his desserts, especially the little cartons of trifle.

They had to carry away the empty cartons so the arog wouldn't know they had eaten them. When he came back to eat his lunch, after he opened his box they could hear him shout out, "For goodness sake she's forgotten to put in my desserts, that's the third day running she's done that."

The four loved their times with the outsiders, they wished it would never end, and almost forgot about the big move coming. Every night they went into the house, something new was in it and the outsiders had to explain what they were. Lots of different arogs they had never seen before were coming to the site now, and they could hear hammering and drilling all day long. Some were carrying items in. Every day was exciting, but for how much longer?

CHAPTER SIXTEEN

THE BLUEBELL FESTIVAL

One day a year was the bluebell festival. Lots of bluebells grew in and around the wood and when they were in full bloom, the queen without any warning would get up early, and stand in the middle of the clearing wearing a new bluebell costume, in the style of that year's fashion. Then the elves had a couple of hours to create something made out of bluebells only – clothes, toys, ornaments, bags, wheelbarrows, etc. Then Bronwen would pick the winner.

The bluebells were only a few days short of full bloom, and she wanted the festival to take place before they moved, so the day before out she came, dressed up, and announced that they only had two hours to complete their entry, as they had to do it before the arogs came.

Rhiannon was very good at designing but her speciality was making hats out of foxgloves. And every year the winner would get one of Rhiannon's special foxglove hats as a prize. They looked great but didn't last long.

Egryn made a pretend catapult out of bluebells, which was hopeless as it collapsed when he fired it. Iori made his in the shape of a buzzard, Iwan a model of the stretcher they used, and Gruffydd designed a model of a chug chug. Because it was used to save Selwyn's life, Bronwen picked Iwan's stretcher as the winner.

For the younger ones, there was a treasure hunt. A special bluebell was hidden somewhere in the forest, or in the clearing usually, but this year it was hidden in one of the trees. It was considered to be too dangerous to have them wandering around on the ground, especially with the dog wandering on his lead. This kept the little ones occupied, whilst the older ones got on with creating their entries.

Selwyn was feeling a bit better, so they positioned him sitting up in a branch so that he could see what was going on.

These goings on took their minds off things, and everyone for a short while forgot what was really about to happen. When the arogs arrived they soon got reminded that this was probably the last time they would play in their settlement.

Bronwen realized this, so that evening she got everyone to eat a larger than normal supper and organized the packing of food they had stored, wrapping things like acorns in various leaves.

Bompa, the only fat elf, who loved food, ate so much he had a massive burp. Everything in his stomach shot up into his mouth. Einion who was sitting on a branch underneath him, got plastered head to foot with really smelly, watery sick and was forced to go to the pond and wash his body and all his clothes. But he still smelt horrible the next day.

MOVING

The sad but exciting moving day arrived. They had so much to do. Little saplings from their trees were cut off, and put into wooden pots at the last minute, ready to be planted as soon as they arrived in their new woods. As Egryn, Iwan and Gruffydd were not moving, and didn't have to carry anything but their catapults, they went ahead as scouts to make sure everything was clear. Especially looking skywards.

Brenig told everyone that he firmly believed that one day they would all be back, and to think of this as a long holiday. I don't think he really believed they would, though. What he didn't say was that the outsiders told him that they had a plan that might work.

Luckily the sun was shining; they waved goodbye to the red squirrels and told them to come and visit. They said, "No way! Don't get friends with the grey ones."

"We won't," they replied.

A couple of pairs of robins decided to go with them.

It was a dangerous journey and twice the scouts shouted

out, "Get under cover!" They dived under ferns, bushes and even brambles. Luckily a buzzard just circled high above them for a few minutes and eventually they were able to continue.

When Egryn finally got back, it seemed so empty, especially without Iori, Alis Hâf and Rhiannon, and he felt really sad. His eyes starting getting darker, but the outsiders saw him, and knew they had to take his mind off things. Gruffydd held a large, long, funny, yellow soft thing, which he said you could eat. It had a skin, and he peeled it back and nibbled a bit.

"Yummy yummy, try some."

Egryn asked, "What is it? Love the smell."

"It's a fruit, called a banana."

Iwan gave him a new one. He nibbled a bit and stated that it was horrible and they laughed as he nibbled the skin; he forgot Iwan had peeled it first.

"Eat the inside only," they told him. He did, and liked it.

The outsiders told them to get moving, as the arog would be there soon and the one with the red hair usually had a bag of thin potato things called crisps in his box. "Let's go and see," remarked Gruffydd, "I wonder what flavour he will have today?"

They went after he arrived to look, but disappointingly the bag was empty – he had eaten them. They were a bit too late.

"Never mind, we will try again tomorrow," explained Iwan, "he has different flavours every day. Hang on, what's this?" In another box was a big orange thing, like a football. Egryn picked that up, smelt it, it seemed OK and was just about to take a bite when they shouted, "No, not yet, that's the outside! You dopey Dan, you nearly did it again."

They dug their fingers in, and peeled a bit of orange skin off. Egryn bit a little bit and said it was juicy, and opened his mouth wide and took a huge bite. The next second he hurt his teeth on something hard. It was the pip.

Iwan said, "You've got to be careful as sometimes these pips are inside, like an apple."

It was a funny day. The settlement seemed so empty. Egryn kept expecting to see some of the others in their trees. That night Egryn slept with the other two in Brenig's tree. It was a strange, funny feeling – everything was so quiet. He wondered what Iori was doing in his new home, and wished he was here. He never slept much. It was a long night and it seemed ages until the morning came.

CHAPTER EIGHTEEN

THE ATTACK

Egryn decided he might as well get up even earlier as he couldn't sleep, and was just going to go out when he heard a shout from a red squirrel.

"Egryn, wake up! There's one coming, a grey squirrel has entered our woods!"

Egryn got his catapult and rushed out. He watched as the grey squirrel sniffed around all the trees, and then went back where he came from. The red squirrel was shaking like a leaf. The outsiders had now woken and saw the grey squirrel leave, and Iwan explained, "He is on a scouting mission, and must now know that the woods are pretty empty. He will, I think, be back soon with his gang, probably tonight, just when it's starting to get dark and after the arogs have gone."

"Oh no!" shouted out another red squirrel, who had appeared shaking like a leaf. "We must run away as far as possible, and as quickly as possible, before the greys come back. Come on, get whatever you can carry and let's go, now!"

But Iwan told them, "Hold your horses." Whatever that meant. "Don't go. Get inside Brenig's tree trunk and don't worry, you must not leave this wood because that's just what the greys want. Meanwhile we have to plan. Right Gruffydd, you see if you can find any boxes of small nails the arogs have stored anywhere. Egryn, you go and get some brambles, and start blocking that gap between these trees to stop the greys coming through there. I think you can start doing that now, as the arogs can't see that bit from the house, but be careful. I'm going to get some ammunition for the catapults and some vines to make traps. As soon as the arogs have gone, work as fast as you can as the greys might come earlier."

Gruffydd told the reds to get as high as they could and to find a spot with an escape route along the branches, just in case the worst happened.

Iwan pondered. "So let's see, if Egryn blocks that way, Gruffydd puts the nails from the arogs' box there on the road as soon as the arogs have gone, I can set the traps and snares for that bit, and that leaves only that gap between those two trees as the only way they can come. Let's go. No time to waste."

When the arogs had gone, they got on with the job immediately. The reds were too scared to move from their treetop hideout, so the robins were sent to watch out in case the greys came earlier. Gruffydd got some nails and spread them pointing upwards out of the ground. The other gaps were blocked with brambles and traps, and the three of them positioned themselves so that they could all fire down from the branches from three different directions at the one spot which they would have to come through.

They had nearly finished setting everything up when the robins came chirping madly. Iwan shouted, "Leave everything and get into position."

The catapults and ammunition were awaiting them in their spot. Next, they heard shouts of pain, as lots of greys, too many to count, came along the path and trod on some nails. They turned back and tried another way but this one was blocked by the thick brambles. Trying a third way, two greys trod on the trap and their legs got tangled in vines. It took them a while to chew them to get them out. They now realized that there was only one other way to get into their woods. They headed for the gap which they had spied. All going to plan so far.

That's exactly what the elves thought would happen. The ambush had been set. Immediately the three elves shot their catapults continuously at them, and lots of greys screamed in pain as they were hit by flying nuts and conkers.

One of the young reds was curious and leant over the edge of the branch to see what was happening. Unfortunately, he went a little too far as the thin branch gave way under his weight, and he fell head first towards the ground. They were not sure if that killed him, because instantly a grey dashed over to him and bit him in the neck and that was definitely a killer blow.

The shooting continued endlessly and the greys were stopped in their tracks.

The leader of the greys shouted, "Get back!" and in their panic two greys went the wrong way and almost bumped into the dog, who heard the noise and was straining at the end of his lead to break away. The greys turned and all ran away as fast as they could.

"They won't be back, I don't think," remarked Iwan, "but just in case let's start collecting some more ammunition. Remember, at first light we must remove the traps in case any friendly animals get trapped."

Egryn went to tell the reds the good news but they decided to stay where they were for the rest of the day, as they were still too scared to move. They asked the elves to bury the young red one who had died. They did this straight away.

Before they went to sleep they had a debate about who was the best shot with the catapult. Gruffydd said, "If we had bows and arrows we could have shot further," but Iwan replied, "They are more dangerous and designed to kill, so have been banned for hundreds of years. I'm not sure how to fire them properly."

Gruffydd said, "We've seen them used by a few wild elves. We've had a little practice shooting them ourselves. We can show you if you want?"

"Perhaps one day," replied Egryn. "All I can say is thank goodness you two outsiders were still here, as I could never have turned them all back on my own. I didn't realize there were so many grey squirrels living so close to our settlement. There never used to be any, anywhere near. Everything is changing for the worse."

CHAPTER NINETEEN

THE WORKERS LEAVE

The next day there was a hub of activity, as the arogs looked like they were tidying up and loading the chug chugs. The dog was taken off his lead and one chug chug went off with him. This might be the last day they could sneak items out of the lunch boxes, so they took twice as much as normal.

At lunchtime they heard a noise, as two arogs were quarrelling. One accused the other of stealing food from his box. One said, "I definitely had two packets of crisps, prawn cocktail and salt and vinegar, in my box, and now they are gone. You greedy guzzler, eat your own!"

The other announced, "I haven't touched your lousy grub. Anyway, I've got a packet of Quavers missing as well. Have you had those?"

"No, I haven't. You are making that up because you pinched mine."

"Rubbish, I never did. You are going off your head. You probably never had any in the first place."

"I did, you lying pig!"

"What did you call me?"

"You heard!"

"Right that's it, I've had a gutsfull of you, you big slob!" and he shoved him over.

The three elves watched from the tree as the two arogs rolled about on the ground, wrestling each other.

Eventually the boss of the arogs came over, broke up the fight and ordered them to get into the chug chug, which they did.

So the three of them hid high up in the furthest tree and watched the chug chugs leave, probably for the last time. They opened the packets they had pinched. The first one was the Quavers; they melted in their mouths and they said they all liked them. The second one was prawn cocktail. The two outsiders had a bit and said they were rather strong but they would eat them if they were hungry.

Egryn smelt it and said, "No way I'm eating that smelly thing, bit like fish."

Next was salt and vinegar, and they all had to have a drink of raspberry juice as they burnt their tongues on the sharp taste.

Peeping through the leaves after hearing the sound of a zoom zoom, Iwan could see a new one coming. They had never seen this one before and it pulled up in front of the house. They watched as two adult arogs, and a little young one got out. They had never seen these before.

Gruffydd decided to get as near as possible to try and hear what they were saying, as he could understand some arogs' speech.

He heard the female arog say, "Well, Gwyn, what do you think of your new house?" and the little one ran up to the door and tried to push it open.

"Wait for me to unlock it." The male one strode up to the door and inserted a key.

The three of them went into it and Gruffydd scurried back, telling them the news. After about half an hour the three came back out, and they heard an arog say that everything would be cleared away by the end of tomorrow. They had been given a set of keys and told the house would be theirs tomorrow morning. They were also told that the fence on either side would be put up, they hadn't forgotten about it. After a short while the three arogs came out, locked the door and got in and drove away. The three elves watched them disappear in the distance and realized it would be the last time they could go inside the empty house.

"Come on you lot," shouted Iwan, "no time to waste!"

They scurried down and went in through the letterbox.

Gruffydd announced, "It's sailing time!" They headed up to the bathroom. They saw there was now a carpet on the stairs.

"Wait a minute, we need boats," stated Iwan. Egryn told them to start the water flowing as he would get some. He went out through the letterbox and got three big leaves. The bath wasn't deep enough yet, so he took the leaves to the top of the stairs, placed them down and told Gruffydd to open the lounge door fully. He went on a leaf first, pushed off and slid down really fast, bumping on the end of each step, swerving at the bottom and going through the lounge, to slow down just before crashing into the kitchen door. They all had a few goes but were a bit sore, so Iwan got the bath ready and they then used the leaves as rafts and had raft races.

When they finally decided to go back to the tree to sleep, as it was getting late, they were just about to go out the letterbox when Gruffydd said, "Let's have a last ride down the drainpipe!"

Egryn instantly stated, "That's a good idea, but I've got a better one. We have never slept in an arog's house, and this might be our last chance to do it before they move in. What do you think?"

They all agreed it was good idea. They each found a nice soft spot on the carpet, and didn't need any blankets as it was warm inside.

Before they cwtched down Iwan said, "I'm always the first to wake at first light, so when I do I will wake you up as we must then go out as we've got a meeting with the mole family first thing. Also I need to get lots of dead worms as a gift for them."

Egryn asked, "Why are we having a meeting?" and Iwan answered, "It's a surprise, as I want them to do a job for me before we leave tomorrow."

Egryn was shocked as he didn't realize how fast the days had gone, and asked them if they really had to go.

Gruffydd replied, "We don't like staying too long in one place, we are adventurers, we need to move on. Don't worry, we will come back every now and then when we are in this area."

So they all laid down and tried to sleep on the carpet, but they found it too itchy and stuffy and in the end the three of them got up and left to go and sleep in the tree in the fresh, cooling air. Iwan's legs were bleeding because he had scratched them so much.

CHAPTER TWENTY

MOVING IN

Morris the mole arrived very early next morning, as he was scared of arogs.

"Good gracious m-me," he remarked. "What's happened to this p-place? There's never been a house here ever. What can I do for you t-two as I owe you a f-favour?"

"Yes you certainly do. Come, follow me and we will show you."

Egryn went as well as he was curious. They took Morris to the spot where the pond was, and he was shocked at seeing that tons of earth had been dumped on top of it. They explained that they wanted Morris to dig a tunnel from the furthest trench to the pond. Then tunnels to the second and third unfilled trench. Morris reminded them that he hated water – he could certainly dig a tunnel from that trench almost to the pond, but they must do the last bit as he didn't want a soaking.

"Why do you want me to do it?" he inquired.

"Our plan is to flood the trenches and stop any more houses being built. Also it might make the other house damp, and they might decide to leave and not continue to build them. Anyway it's worth a try."

"That's fine, no problem. It might work, good plan!"

"How long do you think it will take?" inquired Gruffydd.

"I will probably finish it by early t-tomorrow," Morris remarked.

"Why do you say some letters twice?" inquired Iwan.

"Oh he's always had a stutter, lot's of moles do it. It's because they don't speak much, not used to it," explained Egryn.

"Well that's OK, Egryn you can do the last bit as we are off gallivanting in about half an hour."

"As soon as that, can't you at least stay till tonight?" Egryn pleaded.

"No, once we decide to go, we go."

They presented Morris with some dead worms they had found for his breakfast, and he gobbled them down. He was just going to start digging, when the two outsiders stood up and said their goodbyes quickly, before striding off into the distance, with barely a glance back. Just before they got out of hearing distance Egryn shouted to remind them to call in and send Iori if they saw him.

They replied, "Will do. We're off to get some wild strawberries first. See you in a few weeks perhaps," and disappeared from view.

Morris retorted that he couldn't hang about, he hated sunlight, and in about a minute he had disappeared into a hole in the ground.

Egryn felt really lonely as, until the mole surfaced whenever he felt like it, probably hours later, he had nobody to talk to, and nobody to have fun with. But he felt he had made real friends with two exciting characters who he hoped would be back a lot. What an exciting life they must have.

He climbed the highest tree to see if he could still see the two outsiders, and while he was looking he could see a zoom zoom coming, and a chug chug behind.

Within minutes they pulled up in front of the house, the same couple and young boy. What was his name now? Gwyn I think. He got out and the huge chug chug pulled up behind and two arogs got out and opened the back door of their chug chug, and climbed in.

Meanwhile, the family walked up to the front door, put in the key and walked in. The other two arogs, whom they hadn't seen before, then unloaded the chug chug and kept carrying items into the house. Egryn was fascinated and watched as he had never seen what arogs had in their house. Looked like chairs, tables, big soft seats, and many, many boxes. After a while the lady arog came to the door with the boy, passed him a big round thing, and told him to play football on the grass, which he did. He was kicking the big round thing with his foot and was aiming between two trees then shouting, "Goal!"

Egryn enjoyed watching him and decided to get a bit nearer, so he got down from the high branches and settled on one, just above where he was kicking. The boy was running underneath him and eventually stopped kicking and sat down on the grass.

Egryn stayed absolutely still, and studied the boy's hair, clothes, shoes etc. He was told by Brenig that he was not to be seen. He must have no contact with any arog, not even a young one.

Then the lady arog came out and told Gwyn something, and he got up and went inside, but left the big round thing in the garden. Egryn couldn't go down and touch it as the arogs were continuously going back in to the house carrying items. This went on for ages, and Egryn had to keep glancing to the side to see if Morris would be coming up out of his tunnel, as he didn't know the arogs had arrived.

After a while, the lady came out with a box, put it on the grass and told Gwyn to play there as it was safer and the arogs wouldn't be long, then he could come back in. Egryn watched as he got out little tiny chug chugs, and zoom zooms, made noises and played with them on the grass. Not long after another box was brought out from the chug chug and the lady told the arogs to put it by Gwyn, not to bring it in.

Egryn was amazed as Gwyn kept putting his hand in the box and bringing out what looked like little people, all dressed differently. Gwyn would have one in each hand and pretend they were having a fight. Egryn loved watching this as Gwyn kept making fighting noises. Each one had a name, strange ones like The Undertaker and Triple H.

Eventually the two arogs came out, shut the back door of the chug chug and drove off. The lady came out and told Gwyn to come in and see his new bedroom. Not long after, it started getting dark and Egryn nearly jumped out of his skin when lights came on in the rooms, and the garden was lit up as if it was still daylight.

Morris then poked his head up and said he was shattered, and would finish the job in the morning. He heard the chug chug coming as he could also feel the vibrations under ground, so he carried on working until he heard it go away. But he looked at the lights and said it hurt his eyes, and announced that he was going to sleep in his brand new tunnel, which he did, after promising to finish the other tunnels joining the trenches first thing in the morning.

Egryn got up his tree and wondered whether to sleep in Brenig's as it was much bigger, and had a huge hollowed trunk. However, he decided against it. However it was no use, it was too quiet, and the lights were still on in the house. If he got on a certain branch he could see in the upstairs windows, and noticed one room looked like it was for Gwyn, as he was bouncing up and down on his new bed, and his head kept appearing in the window. Egryn watched as Gwyn's head could be seen every few seconds as he bounced up. This went on until his mam came in and drew the curtains and he couldn't see any more. But he still couldn't sleep as he was too excited. Not even when all the lights went off, but he must have eventually as he woke up and it was morning.

CHAPTER TWENTY-ONE

HAVING RIDES

It was much safer wandering around on the ground if he wanted, now that the dog was gone. Still, to be on the safe side he jumped from a branch on his tree to an adjoining branch a few times, and got to Brenig's tree, which he knew had a pile of nuts stored from last year. He took a handful and found the best branch to watch the front of the house without being seen.

The sun had only been up a short while before he saw Gwyn's curtains being drawn, and he was standing on the bed looking out. *Funny* he thought, *he seems to be looking straight at me. He can't be. With my changing coloured hair and clothes that camouflage me in the trees, and being so small and a good bit away, he can't possibly see me.* But he didn't move just in case. Still it appeared as if Gwyn was staring at him. It was very unnerving.

Every now and then he could see some loose earth appearing on the surface and remembered about Morris. It looked like he'd almost finished, as the earth was appearing between the second and third trench.

Suddenly the door opened, a male arog came out and strode towards his zoom zoom, and got in. The female arog and little boy waved to him from the doorway as he drove away.

Behind the house Egryn could see a metal thing sticking out of the ground, and he wondered what it was. It wasn't there yesterday and he had never seen one before. He saw that it was for drying clothes, as the lady came out with a basket full of wet ones and pulled down four bits of metal with lines joining them. Egryn watched as Gwyn passed some little things to his mam, and she used them to fix the clothes to the lines. There was a little breeze and the line started moving around in a circle. Seemed clever. Good way to get them dry. *It would be great if Iori, Rhiannon and Alis Hâf were here, as we could all have rides on it.* He realized that the stronger the wind blew, the faster it revolved.

After the two went back in Egryn looked to see if everything was clear, and made his way towards the centre pole. He easily climbed up and balanced along to what the arogs called a sock, and climbed in, and had a lovely ride as the sock went around and around. This was great fun and he wondered how fast it could go around when the wind was really, really blowing. As the line slowed when the breeze eased he could see Morris emerging from the hole in the ground, and could see he was looking for Egryn, but he had poor eyesight and could hardly see him if he was standing next to him.

Getting down and off, Egryn made his way to Morris. "There you are," he said. "I've f-finished," he stuttered, "and all you have to do is to move this little s-stone and the water will trickle out into the first trench. It might take ages, but eventually the first trench will fill, then the s-second and then even on to the built h-house."

He said, "I'm going to have a little n-nap in the tunnel as the daylight makes my eyes sleepy, and then I will probably wander around looking for s-some worms. After that, another nap. When it starts to get dark I will make my way to my proper maze of tunnels. So it's goodbye then. If you have any problems with the trenches filling up with mud let me know. You can find me under the old y-yew tree next to the big round r-rock when it's a full moon."

After saying all that in the hole, he disappeared.

CHAPTER TWENTY-TWO

WATCHING WRESTLING

It was a nice, sunny day. Egryn heard the back door open, and the mam came out with a big box, followed by Gwyn. She told him to play with his wrestlers on that bit of grass, and she went back in and got a blanket and placed it on the ground, and lifted the box on to it.

"Tomorrow it will be even better," she remarked, "for the men are coming to finish laying the artificial grass and put up the fences. It will be nice and soft for you to play on, and your wrestlers won't get muddy."

She left the door ajar in case Gwyn wanted to come in.

Egryn had to find the best spot to watch, and made his way around in a circle until he was in a bush about three metres from Gwyn.

For half an hour he watched and listened as Gwyn picked some of these so-called wrestlers up, and had one in each hand, pretending they were having a fight. They all had different names, such as The Undertaker, Roman Reigns, the Hardy Brothers and Gwyn's favourite who always seemed to win, John Cena. He watched, fascinated, as Gwyn lifted a wrestling ring from the box and announced to himself that this next wrestling fight was to be for the world championship, and was between John Cena and Triple H. He had one in each hand and proceeded to enact a match, commentating loudly. Egryn enjoyed watching him. Somehow he could understand some of the words he spoke. Bit like elfish.

Suddenly Gwyn stopped mid-fight and appeared to be staring straight at Egryn. He didn't move an inch but still Gwyn stared at him and spoke softly.

"Pwy wyt ti?"

How can he speak elfish? That translated as "Who are you?"

Egryn decided to not to answer, and Gwyn put down the two wrestlers and moved closer to the bush. He then said, *"Gwelais i chi neithiwr. Peidiwch a rhedeg i ffwrdd."*

This was more elfish again, meaning, "I saw you last night and I don't want you to run away." Gwyn lifted his hand, moved a bit of the bush aside so he could see Egryn properly. Should he try and run away? He must not be seen. *Arogs don't know we exist. Must not know about us. Better to remain perfectly still.*

He hesitated, and Gwyn said that he would move back if he would come out of the bush, and let him see him properly. That's exactly what he did; he moved back and sat on the new artificial grass which felt funny, and indicated for Egryn to come out of the bush and stand in front of him. Egryn panicked. He jumped out of the bush and ran as fast as he could to the nearest tree, and was up high in the branches in the blink of an eye.

Gwyn got up and called out that he wanted to be his friend, and to prove it would leave a nice surprise under the bush in the morning. He then went in and Egryn jumped across the branches, got to his own tree and snuggled down inside the trunk.

He had a lot of thinking to do. How had the boy seen him, and how could the boy speak a language that is almost the same as elfish?

It spotted with rain so the little boy didn't come out again, but his mam did, to pick up the box of toys and wrestling ring. He had forgotten all about the stone and the tunnels and wondered how many days it would be before Iori Llew came to stay, as he said he would after he had settled in.

Eventually the zoom zoom came back, the man carried out a box from the boot, and when Gwyn came out of the door his dad said that he'd got a surprise for him in the morning. Soon the lights came on again, just like the night before and eventually hours later, off, and everything went quiet. Egryn was dying to look through the window, but was too scared to go closer and the curtains were closed, so he couldn't now even if he wanted too. Egryn went to sleep feeling a mixture of being scared, amazed, shocked, worried and puzzled.

CHAPTER TWENTY-THREE

TRAPPED IN

As soon as the sun rose, Egryn woke as usual. It took him a while before he realized he was alone, and peeped out of a branch. He saw that Gwyn's curtains were still drawn. So he ate some food and got to the top of the tree to see where the red squirrels were, jumped away from branch to branch to their tree, and told them about the little boy who saw him. The squirrels said he should never go near the house again, and to keep away from all arogs, even little ones.

Seymour stated, "It's too dangerous. You won't find us anywhere near that house or garden. Arogs are killers. We are never going to that side of the wood again. You should do the same. Believe me."

He made his way back, wondering if he should follow their advice, when he saw the male arog come out of the house with the box he had brought home. For the next half hour he saw him build up something which went back and forth with a seat on it. The arog pushed it back and forward, tested to see if it was firmly in the ground then went to the door and shouted to Gwyn to come out. As he got to the door he saw his new swing for the first time.

His dad said that it was a welcome present for his new house, lifted him up and pushed him, so he shot up in the air. The more he pushed the higher he got, and Egryn wondered if he would go all the way upside down, but he never did. After a while his dad said he must make it go himself by leaning back and pulling on the ropes – he tried and managed it a bit. His dad said with practice he would get better and go high on his own, but he must leave now to go to work. Which he did.

Gwyn played on his own, practising going back and forth, until he became quite good at it. He decided to swing high from a sitting position then jump off. Where he landed, he got a leaf and marked the spot. He tried then to break his record, and if he went further he moved the leaf. After about ten goes he stood up, looked at the tree in which Egryn was watching and inquired, "I hope you enjoyed watching me jump?"

Egryn was startled. He decided to say nothing and very, very slowly moved back in the tree, barely moving. He pondered on the fact he was seen again, and the fact that he could understand what he said. Looking down at his clothes he could see everything was normal, no arog should be able to see him among leaves, not even from even a close distance.

Gwyn then went in and came out with a different box. Egryn didn't know that they were Toy Story figures and Gwyn played with them until his mam came out, and told him he must come in to have his dinner.

No sooner had he gone in than Egryn came down and crawled over to the box. He didn't know whether to touch any of them, and didn't know if they moved. He poked his finger at a button on the end of one of them and had a shock when it announced, "I am Buzz Lightyear, to infinity and beyond."

Egryn sprinted away and shot up the tree like a bullet. He thought they were toys; he didn't know they were real and could talk. Remember Egryn had never touched an arog or ever owned anything made out of plastic. He didn't know what a battery was.

Gwyn never came out again for the rest of the day as it was showering, and his mam took the box in. When his dad came back his mam came out with Gwyn and his dad told them to hurry up, as he was starving and yelled, "McDonald's here we come!"

Egryn watched the car leave, made his way over to the swing and clambered up onto the seat but it was no good; he couldn't move it, he wasn't heavy enough. The wind moved it a bit, so he had to go to sit on the end to hold the rope. Still, he enjoyed it but it only moved about six inches.

Looking at the house, he wondered whether it would be a good idea to go in. Perhaps just a quick look around. There was nobody inside.

Getting through the letterbox, he noticed that everything had changed. There were lots more items in the rooms. *Bet Gwyn's room will be the most interesting*, he thought, so he pondered on deciding which window Gwyn had peeped out of and guessed it was up the stairs and to the left. The easiest way to get up was along the banister and lucky for him, that bedroom had its door ajar. He squeezed around the door and saw that the floor was almost completely covered with clothes and books and toys. Really messy. Bit like Iori's.

Looking at the bed, he could see that it was covered by a blanket with toy pictures on it, including that one who said he was Buzz Lightyear. There were a stack of boxes built into a cupboard, which wasn't closed properly, and when he peeped in one he could see this Buzz. So he poked him then jumped back, and hid behind the leg of the bed. Nothing happened. He never came after him. Going back, he peeped in and saw he had never moved. Therefore he pressed the button again and Buzz said the same words. Egryn realized he must be able to speak but somehow was not real. He wondered how that was possible. Also he was hard, not soft like an elf. When he tapped him, he made a noise. Very odd.

Looking up he could see tall cupboards; one had its door wide open and was full of clothes. Touching them was strange as none of them were made out of leaves, rushes or fruits of the trees. Not an acorn hat in sight. They felt a bit rough and had a horrible, unnatural smell.

In one corner was a model of a wooden building and it was full of model zoom zooms and chug chugs. If you pushed them, they moved. Egryn was intrigued by a little room which moved up and down on a string when you turned a lever. If you put a zoom zoom inside it you could move it up to the roof. Then you could push it down a ramp and it would speed across the carpet. Great fun.

Fascinated by this, he didn't hear the family come back, and the next thing he knew the front door had opened. Gwyn was told to go up and change out of his best clothes;

he dashed up the stairs, and Egryn just had time to hide behind the curtain before he charged through the door like a bull through a gate. Lucky he wasn't behind it.

Gwyn changed very quickly because he wanted to get downstairs, as his favourite programme *Sam Tân (Fireman Sam)* was coming on and rushing out, he slammed the door behind him. After hearing his feet stamping down the stairs, Egryn came out from behind the curtain, saw it was clear, and was dismayed when he saw the door was closed.

Therefore he must get out of the window, but climbing up he saw they were all closed and the handles were too heavy for him to budge. He was trapped. He must get out as he couldn't imagine sleeping inside this stuffy arog house. Having a cooling breeze on his face all night while he slept was what he was used to. Also the smell; no leaves, fruits, flowers, grass, trees, bushes, berries but horrible dry, dusty air. He had only been in a short while and he felt like coughing all the time.

The only chance perhaps was to stand next to the door, and as Gwyn opened it, to nip out before he slammed it shut. There was bound to be a window open somewhere else in the house. Or he could go downstairs and out of the letterbox, but that was a bit risky. In the meantime it was so stuffy, he felt he must get off this carpet and get higher up. But he couldn't go far as he must be near the door when Gwyn came back.

Next to the door was a short set of drawers, so he climbed up and knew that he could jump down, land softly on the carpet, and be by the door in seconds. He waited. The time seemed to go so slowly, he dare not move but he was bored stiff. Sitting on the edge, dangling his legs, he studied the room. On the wall were large posters of wrestlers, they looked so nasty and on another it had printed out *Plentyn yr Wythnos* (Child of the Week). Egryn couldn't read it; there was no need for elves to write letters.

Another wall had a poster of a funny blue chug chug on rails. He had a big round smiling face with the letters *Tomos Y tanc. Never seen one of those before. I wonder how many different chug chugs and zoom zooms there are.*

It was so boring Egryn decided he had to get down. He decided not to jump all the way but from one drawer handle down to another, and so on. Another set of drawers at the other end of the room had the bottom one half open, so he decided to have a peep in. Getting up, he could see it looked like the things he saw Gwyn wear on his feet. Lots of them. He leant over to feel what they were like, leant too far and fell in but luckily they were so soft it cushioned his fall. *Great. This is fun.* He continuously got back up and jumped in, getting more confident and even doing somersaults. He did a double one, and eventually after jumping up higher a triple somersault. This meant he crashed down almost to the bottom of the draw and at that very moment he could hear footsteps coming up the stairs.

Scrambling up, he jumped on the floor and dashed for the edge of the door but he was too late. As he was halfway towards the door it opened. Egryn stopped still, scared stiff and could see Gwyn standing in the doorway, staring at him. He was too scared to move as this giant (or so it seemed to him) closed the door.

Gwyn spoke softly and in a language which Egryn could mostly make out, told him not to be scared as he wouldn't harm him. To prove it, he said that he would open the door and stand aside so he could get out, but first Gwyn just wanted him to answer a few questions. That's exactly what he did. Egryn could go if he wanted but he was unsure; as the boy had a happy, smiling face, obviously didn't want to harm him and had stood aside, he just stood perfectly still. To ease the tension Gwyn told Egryn his name and asked what his name was. He didn't answer but Gwyn asked again.

"Egryn," he whispered in a shaky, nervous voice.

"Oh great, a good old Welsh name like mine."

Now that he had answered, Gwyn blurted out a rush of questions and asked what he was, where he lived, if there were any more of him, etc.

Before he could answer, Egryn coughed.

Gwyn asked him what the matter was, and Egryn stammered that it was too stuffy and his mouth was dry. Understanding him, he went over to the window and before he opened it he said that he could go out, he wouldn't stop him but tomorrow morning after breakfast, he would stand under the yew tree and wait for him.

Egryn didn't reply but raced to the window, went out like a flash, jumped up to the shute, ran inside it to the drainpipe, and down to the ground. There were no ferns at the bottom this time so when he landed, he hurt his bum. As he struggled up, rubbing his bum, Gwyn's head peeped out of the window and saw him dash towards the trees.

Egryn was completely out of breath when he got high up into safety, and couldn't sit down as his bum was still hurting. He had lots to think about; he made his way to his own tree and gingerly sat down.

Lots to think about. The boy arog did let him go. *He now knows I live in the woods and is bound to come looking for me in the morning. Shall I meet up with him? How can he speak my language and see me? Perhaps I should meet up and find out? Will he tell his parents? What if Brenig finds out?*

Sitting uncomfortably and pondering, he then could just about hear a squirrel approaching. It was Seymour who came towards him and asked him where he had been, because his friend Iori Llew had come to see him. "He waited for hours, but decided to go back before it was dark. I told him I hadn't seen you today. He searched all the trees, looked along the fruit bushes, and even spied on the house. But there was no sign of you. He said he was very disappointed to have missed you."

Both Seymour and Egryn wondered how they would get news to Iori Llew that Egryn was back; they didn't want Iori to give up and not return.

"Anyway, where have you been?" Seymour asked again.

He just answered, "Having an adventure," and moved away. He didn't want to lie, and was too tired to think properly.

Egryn had so much going on in his head he couldn't concentrate on anything, so he thought it was a good idea to have an early night, and decide what to do in the morning.

CHAPTER TWENTY-FOUR

WOODY IN THE WINDOW

The next day it was pouring down. Elves are not fussy about the rain but they don't get wet, as their clothes are made out of a mixture of leaves and rushes and the water just runs off. Lots of them wear hats fashioned out of acorns, and they know every spot in every tree which stays dry. The ground being wet is a nuisance. Looking at the rain, Egryn realized that the tunnels had been built; he had forgotten about Morris.

What should he do? Should he go and check Morris's work and possibly move the stone, should he leave and go and see Iori Llew, or hide by the tree in case the boy came, or ignore him and avoid him? Would the boy come out in the rain anyway?

He wanted to talk to someone, so he went to the other end of the woods to see Seymour. The squirrels hated the rain and would be nice and cosy inside their tree. Avoiding the ground and going from branch to branch, he made his way there. He couldn't go in a straight line as there were gaps, but eventually he managed.

Telling Seymour his thoughts, and what had happened the day before, he was advised to avoid the little boy and never go in the house again. They said they would keep away from that side of the wood forever.

Perhaps he was right. But elves are mischievous and like adventures and having fun, so he decided to find a dry spot as near the yew tree as possible, and see if the boy would come. That's what he did. It was boring and the rain was pelting down so he decided to go back to his tree; as he did he happened to glance up at Gwyn's window and saw that he was staring at him. Then he put something up to his eyes, took it back down and waved. How could he possibly be seen from so far, and not be camouflaged by the leaves? He couldn't resist it, he waved back and the boy smiled and waved continuously back to him.

Gwyn then disappeared from the window, and moments later was standing in the middle of the front door. Looking at the rain, he went back in the house and left the front door open. Egryn saw this and wondered if he wanted him to go in. Bit dangerous, as he didn't want to meet the big arogs or get trapped again. He kept hearing Brenig's voice telling him he must not be seen.

Moments later Gwyn appeared, dressed in a long coat with boots on his feet. He stepped out and opened something which he had in his hand, which he placed above his head. Egryn had never seen an umbrella like it, though the elves did fashion similar ones sometimes. Just as the boy stepped out, his mam came to the doorway and told him to "keep the umbrella up, don't go far, don't jump in puddles and be back in the house in ten minutes."

Gwyn came towards his tree and leant on the trunk. He then told Egryn he knew he was there and not to be afraid, he wanted to be his friend, and he promised not to tell anyone about him, not even his parents. Putting something wrapped up against the trunk, he looked up and explained that it was a goodwill present, and if Egryn unwrapped it he should eat it, as he bet he would love it. Also he was going back in, he would leave his bedroom window open at the top, and he was welcome to come and visit.

Egryn didn't reply, and he watched as the boy turned and headed back in. He slid down a branch and landed by the gift. It had been split into four bits, which was handy as it would probably be too heavy. Unwrapping one bit, he nibbled a small piece and loved it. Next he carried that piece up into the tree. Licking away in great delight more and more, he then noticed that the little window in Gwyn's bedroom was now open. After eating that one whole piece of the bar of chocolate he took the rest, one a bit at a time, to his own tree.

"This is so gorgeous, don't be greedy, keep some for another time," he murmured to himself. Storing them carefully inside a leaf and inside the trunk, he then made his way back towards the nearest branch to the front of the house, so that he could see Gwyn's window again.

It was still open and Gwyn was looking out. *Shall I risk it? Perhaps so.* Wondering which way to get in, he could see Gwyn had now spotted him and was signalling for him to come up.

So he did. He couldn't go up inside the pipe as he would get soaked, so he climbed up the outside. It was a bit slower and harder but eventually he got to the little window. He hesitated.

Gwyn, opening the window a little more, exclaimed, "Come on, it's perfectly safe. I've closed the bedroom door, and anyway my mam is downstairs watching *Bargain Hunt.*"

"What's that?"

"It's a programme on what we call a television."

"A television… never heard of it. What is it exactly?"

"Well it's like a box with moving pictures. Never mind about that, come on in as she will be watching it for ages."

Egryn had a good look and then went in and stood inside on the window ledge.

Gwyn then explained that he would stay back a bit and answer any questions he was asked.

The first thing Egryn asked was how could Gwyn speak a language which is almost the same as elfish?

"It's not elfish, it's Cymraeg, it's been spoken in this country for more than a thousand years. It's almost disappeared in England and Scotland but still spoken by a lot of people in Cymru. Here, in what they call Wales, it's named Welsh. It's my family's first language. You will probably not have heard it before as the people who built the house couldn't speak it, they spoke English which you wouldn't understand. It's a new language."

"I can understand lots of it but if you speak a little bit slower I can understand more, but you might have to explain some new words I have never heard of, like television."

"It's a deal."

Egryn then asked, "Another thing which completely mystifies me is how can you see me, even at a distance and I'm supposed to be camoflagued?"

Gwyn replied, "I'm not sure, but it might be because I'm colour blind."

"What does that mean?"

"Well, I get some colours mixed up. Especially reds, greens and browns. You wear those colours a lot. My parents are not colour blind and they haven't seen you. I haven't told them that I have seen you, even though I was dying too. As far as my parents go you don't exist. In fact even though you are standing in front of me, I find it hard to believe you are real. I thought at first you were a toy with batteries in. But obviously you are a real living thing. How many of you are there?"

It was a lot for Egryn to think about. He hesitated. Gwyn turned his head when he heard some music playing downstairs, then told him that soon the programme would finish, and he would be told to go down to eat.

"Egryn, that's your name isn't it, I would like you to stay in this room and I will come back up, as soon as I can. Will you do that?"

Just then Gwyn's mam shouted up for him to come down.

Being still unsure, Egryn replied that he was going now, and before he went Gwyn explained that he had a favourite toy which he called Woody, and he showed it to Egryn. He explained that when it was safe for him to come in he would put Woody in the window.

The programme had ended and Gwyn's mam called up

again for him to come down, now this minute, and Egryn dashed out of the window and made his way back to his tree.

CHAPTER TWENTY-FIVE

EXPLORING THE HOUSE

In his tree Egryn decided that the boy probably was telling the truth and could be trusted, so he decided that he would definitely go back in.

As the next day was a Saturday, Gwyn's dad didn't have to go to work, and the zoom zoom (which Egryn now realized was called a car) was still outside. Looking at the window, there was no sign of Woody, so Egryn got a handful of nuts which he had earlier knocked the shells off with a stone, and nibbled away looking at the window from a tree branch.

The sun was shining, the rain clouds had gone, the light breeze was making a soft tune rustling the leaves. He was dangling his legs to the rhythm of the sound and life was great – well, it nearly always was for an elf.

Something was going on, as he could hear a lot of movement coming from the house, then the door opened and three of them came out. Gwyn glanced up, couldn't see Egryn and wondered which tree he was in. Egryn could see him looking, so he dropped a nut straight down. Gwyn saw it and looked up and spied Egryn, but before he could say anything his dad opened the door for him to get in.

Gwyn asked, "Have I got to go shopping? Can't I stay? It's really boring."

His dad retorted, "No you can't, how old do you think you are? You are far too young to stay on your own. Now get in."

"Come on, if you are good perhaps you can have a surprise," said his mam and they all got in and drove off.

Egryn had a chance to explore the house, especially downstairs now that it had the rooms full. Looking up, he could see Gwyn had deliberately left his little window open, but it was easier to go through the letterbox than go up the pipe. Going through, he used a little twig he had brought with him to wedge the letterbox open, so that he could make a quick getaway, just in case.

Well, for about half an hour he wandered around the downstairs, exploring. All the time listening for the purr of the engine of the returning car. In the lounge there was a bowl of fruit. He recognized an apple and an orange, which needed to be peeled if he remembered correctly, but didn't know what the round spikey thing was and had a little bite. It was immediately spat out as he didn't realize you had to peel it and it hurt his mouth. He found out later it was a kiwi fruit. Most of the cupboards and drawers were too heavy for him to open.

There was a loud noise coming from the kitchen and he was a bit wary about going in. It couldn't be an arog as they had all gone out. Poking his head slowly around a gap in the door, he could see it was coming from a machine downstairs. Going in what they called a kitchen, he moved towards the noise very slowly. It was a big white thing. There was water inside, and as it was swirling around, white bubbles kept appearing. Getting nearer, he could see it was full of arogs' clothes and he sat down and watched it going around, fascinated.

Suddenly it stopped, Egryn jumped up in fright as it started again, and spun around getting faster and faster and louder and louder. He ran to the gap in the door and hid behind. Was there a monster inside? Why did it suddenly get louder and faster? It went on and on and he could see a little light at the top which changed every minute. When the light went from 1 to 0 it slowed, and gradually stopped and so did the noise. Absolutely fascinating.

Because of the noise he hadn't heard the car come back, and when it stopped he could hear the front door was being opened. He couldn't get out of the letterbox, so his only other option was to go upstairs to Gwyn's bedroom, which luckily for him had its door open. He rushed up quickly, expecting any second someone would shout out "What on earth is that!" But he made it safely.

He could hear lots of coming and going, as they were going in and out and bringing bags from the car. Peeping out of the window, he could see Gwyn going towards the swing and sitting on it, and eating something white. When the two parents went in carrying a bag, he got out, clambered up to the shute, and climbed down the outside of the drainpipe as he didn't want another sore bum. Emerging at the bottom, he made his way quickly to the tree nearest the swing and climbed up the back so the parents wouldn't see him if they came out. Sitting on a branch above Gwyn, he was gasping for breath.

Gwyn obviously heard him as he moved from the car and said, "Good morning, do you want some of my ice cream?"

Egryn didn't know what it was, and Gwyn replied that "It's this cold, nice white stuff which I am eating." Egryn didn't want to come down as it was too dangerous but Gwyn explained to him that his parents always sat down and had a cup of coffee after unpacking the food, and would be in the kitchen at the back of the house.

Anyway, just in case he would get off the swing and come around the back of the tree. Which he did. Holding up the cone, Egryn came halfway down and licked a bit of the white stuff with his tongue. "Agh, it's freezing!" Gwyn laughed and said that he would get used to it, and that he should eat a bit of the outside of his Cornetto as well. So he tried again, and knowing that it would be cold, didn't have such a big lick, and mixed it up with a bit of the outside cone and enjoyed it.

Gwyn told him that because he had been a good boy shopping, his mam had bought him a goody bag, and if he came up to his bedroom later on he could have some.

Finishing his Cornetto, he watched Egryn eating the bit he had broken off, then turned around, sitting on the swing the other way around. He encouraged Egryn to come down and sit on his lap as he hadn't studied him carefully. Egryn wasn't sure if he should, it was all still a bit scary. *It's all getting too friendly. He is an arog after all. But he could have trapped me and he didn't.*

Egryn slid down the rope and at the bottom jumped onto Gwyn's lap. Because he sat the wrong way round he couldn't be seen from the house window, even if his parents left the kitchen.

Gwyn just stared and eyed him up and down. The conversation then went as follows:

"How old are you?"

"Forty."

"Forty? You are older than my dad. Have you got any children?"

"Children? Of course not. No, I'm far too young."

"Too young? That doesn't make sense. My dad is nowhere near forty. Do you live on your own?"

"I do now but up till a few weeks ago I didn't."

"Please explain."

That's exactly what he did, and Gwyn felt sad that the building of his house had affected the elf world, and caused everything to change. He told him that he would be his best friend, and would never hurt him, or tell anyone, not even his mam and dad, about him. He said that he would like to meet other elves and would like to help them to adjust to living near arogs.

Just then his mam came out and remarked, "Talking to yourself again I see, you can stay out for another five minutes if you want, then you must come in."

"OK, mam, will do."

Gwyn carried on talking to Egryn and said that for the next two weeks they must meet each other every day, and he would show him how modern things worked in the house, and teach him new words. Egryn asked why just two weeks, and Gwyn told him that they were going away on a holiday for seven days, and then he would be going to school after he came back. He had to explain what a holiday and a school were. By now he was getting used to Gwyn's accent but had to stop him every now and then to explain what certain words meant.

Gwyn's mam then called for him to go in now, as he'd had far more than five minutes. Before he did he reminded Egryn about the signal in the window, and after checking to see if his mam had gone back in, he lifted him in the palm of his hand and placed him at the top of the swing, then ran in.

CHAPTER TWENTY-SIX

THE GOODY BAG

After a few hours, Egryn checked and noticed that the signal was in the window. Should he go back in now that arogs were inside? What did Gwyn have now, what did he call it? A goody bag, he remembered, and thinking how much he enjoyed the chocolate and ice cream, he decided to go in. Perhaps he might have some things like those.

As soon as he went through the window Gwyn's face beamed, and told him to get up on his bed and see what he had placed there. Looking he could see lots of different things to eat. Sweets, Gwyn called them.

"Try some," he suggested, which he did and because to a little elf they were too big to eat a whole one, he took a small portion of a few. He loved them. Gwyn told him not to eat any more as he would be sick, and he would put the rest in what he called his sweet drawer. Doing it, Gwyn informed him that he would leave the drawer open just enough so that Egryn could come in and help himself whenever he felt like it.

For the next half an hour he asked Egryn lots more questions, then it was his turn to answer some. No sooner had he started than he could hear someone coming up the stairs, so he told Egryn to hide under the pillow, which he just did in time before the door opened. His mam asked him what he'd been doing so long upstairs on his own, as she hadn't heard the TV being on. Gwyn spent lots of time in his bedroom, usually watching kids' TV. Thinking quickly, he replied that he was looking at his pop-up books.

"Well that's good," remarked his mam, "better than watching TV. Which one did you like the best?" Thinking quickly, he answered that it was the one about Aladdin and his magic lamp. That's the only one he could think of, as it was the one he saw stacked on the shelf.

"Well that's enough reading tonight, come down for your supper, but first wash your hands."

"OK, mam, will do." She went down, and he went into the bathroom. When he finished washing he quickly popped back in to see Egryn, but when he looked under the pillow he was gone.

Egryn was back in his own tree having sweets for supper. Being an only child, Gwyn was used to playing on his own in the garden or in his bedroom; he had a great imagination and could play talking to himself for hours. He now relished having someone for company even if it was, believe it or not, a real elf.

CHAPTER TWENTY-SEVEN

THE VISITOR

The next day was Sunday and Gwyn was seen playing with a football with his dad in the garden. Egryn watched unseen in a tree, but he had to go further back as a horrible smell of cooking was coming from the house and making him feel sick.

For his dinner Egryn had two beech nuts, a crab apple and the last sweet from Gwyn's goody bag.

Whilst he was finishing eating, he had a visitor. The squirrel came rushing to his tree and informed him that Iori Llew was coming back. He rushed back to his tree just in time to see his friend arrive. Boy was Iori Llew glad to see Egryn. He told him that he thought he was dead as he couldn't find him, and nobody had seen him. He was really worried.

Egryn told him that he would never believe what had happened to him. But before he revealed his adventures, he asked how everyone was settling down in their new surroundings.

"Not very good," replied Iori, "it's all a bit cramped and

not a lot of fruit, and only a small clearing. The other sites are the same. Nobody's happy but so far we're safe."

After Iori's reply he related everything that had happened since Iori left. Iori was shocked. Elves must not be noticed by arogs, they must not know they exist. When he said he had sat on an arog's lap, Iori Llew didn't believe him and told him he was crackers. "All right then, I will show you it's safe," and Egryn took Iori to the nearest tree to the front of the house. Explaining about the toy in the window, he was disappointed it wasn't there, and said that unless it was they shouldn't go in.

"I wasn't anyway," replied Iori, "you will never catch me in there now that it's occupied."

Egryn told him to wait a while, but the toy never appeared and they went back to his tree. Iori and him had a few wooden horns filled with acorn beer which he had brought as a visiting gift, and explained all the happenings about their last few days in more detail. They especially enjoyed reminiscing about the grey squirrels' attack.

Iori told Egryn that the terrible twins Morgan and Meredydd wanted to come to visit, but so far their parents had said no, and so had Brenig who made sure the squirrels kept an eye on them. Now that he knew that Egryn was safe he was going back tomorrow, as Brenig was anxious, and needed to know if he was alright. Also, tomorrow a gang of them were off on a fruit expedition.

Egryn told him that as soon as the fruit gathering expedition was over he must come back as he missed him. He promised he would.

The next morning Iori was off, but before he went he made Egryn go to the spot where Morris had left the stone which needed to be removed for the water to go into the first trench. Iori said that Brenig knew about it, as the outsiders had called in and told him. He was bound to ask him if he had started the flood and remember an elf can't lie, so he would have to tell him if he hadn't.

He said he wouldn't be surprised if they found out he'd been seen by an arog, that they would send elves to bring him away.

If an elf told even a little fib then their face would get redder and redder, and then a deep purple and everyone would know. They get really ill, have a terrible headache and have to lie down for two whole days, then the headache gradually goes. No point lying anyway if everybody knows it's a lie. But if they didn't ask, he hadn't got to say.

Egryn and Iori pushed hard and the stone moved a little bit, and water gradually appeared at the bottom of the first trench. *Right, that's OK, I don't have to lie,* thought Iori about that, and went off straight away before the buzzards came as they tended to fly over the fields between the two forests about that time every day. But still he had to be careful and go the roundabout way along the hedges, promising to be back in about seven days.

CHAPTER TWENTY-EIGHT

SEEING BOOKS

That morning before Gwyn's dad went off to work, a lorry came with a load of wooden fences. Before they were unloaded the arogs were shown exactly where they were to be constructed. Gwyn was told to play on the other side whenever the arogs were working.

They started in the front, and Gwyn came out the back door and played with his wrestlers on a blanket, which had been put down on the damp grass. Egryn wanted to watch the arogs building the fence. At first he was fascinated, but after a while they just did the same thing over and over, so he made his way around to the back. He climbed to the top of the rotating washing line and had a little ride before getting off and hiding behind Gwyn's big plastic container, when he heard a door open.

"There you are then, I've been waiting for you to come. Didn't see you much yesterday."

Egryn explained that he didn't like the horrible smell and asked what is was. Gwyn told him that it was his mam cooking a Sunday dinner. That it was meat making the smell. Egryn asked what meat was. When he heard it was from a dead animal, which the arogs called a cow, which he had seen when on his travels with the outsiders, he was shocked. How could anyone possibly eat a dead animal, he asked, and was even more shocked when he was told they also eat chickens, sheep, pigs, etc.

"*Ych y fi*, that's disgusting."

"No it's not, it tastes lovely."

"Do you kill them before you cook them?"

"No, we roast them alive."

"That's terrible."

"Don't be so stupid, of course they are dead before we cook them."

"Do you use an oven like us?"

"Oh, you've got ovens have you? Do you use gas or electric?"

"What are they?"

"It's a hot metal thing which we put the meat in."

"Good gracious, they must be massive to get a whole cow in. No we use stones placed in the sun."

"Big cow in an oven, you are so stupid, no, we buy much smaller pieces from a supermarket or butchers."

"What are they?"

"Shops."

"Never heard of them."

Gwyn just laughed at his ignorance.

"Also what do you mean buy?"

"We hand over money."

"What's money?"

"I can't believe you've never heard of money. I will

explain later. Guess what I've got in my pocket?"

"No idea."

Talking of food, Gwyn put his hand in his pocket and brought out a packet of sweets. Unwrapping the fruit pastilles, he took the top one and passed it to Egryn, who liked the look of it and grabbed it. It was so heavy he fell over, and Gwyn laughed so much that his mam came out and asked what he was laughing at. Luckily Egryn had fallen behind the box.

Anyway his mam told him that he must come in as the workmen were coming around to the back garden shortly, as they couldn't do the fence or grass there last week because of the rain.

So she lifted up his box of wrestlers, and Egryn had to dive in very quickly and hide behind some. It was very scary – would she see him? Lucky the box was all bodies, legs and arms. She carried it in through the door and Gwyn followed, and his mam said that it would be better to go upstairs as she was going to hoover. He could watch the TV in his bedroom if he wanted.

So Egryn had a nice ride up and got out when the coast was clear. Gwyn then gave him a tour of his bedroom, showing what was in all the cupboards and wardrobes. Egryn couldn't understand why he had so many clothes.

Showing him his bookshelf, he remarked that the Aladdin one was his favourite and he put it on the floor in front of Egryn. Turning over the pages of the big pop-up book, Egryn stared at the images, but when Gwyn turned a page and a giant image of the genie popped up Egryn screamed, and ran and hid under the bed. Gwyn laughed and turned over a few more, and eventually Egryn came back over and was told to touch the pictures as they were only paper, and popped down when the page was turned. Gwyn decided to put the TV on to mask any sounds they made.

Gradually Egryn got used to seeing the pictures pop up. His favourite one was the Peter Pan book, when a massive pirate ship zoomed up. He had never seen or heard of the sea and Gwyn had to explain it to him, remembering to speak slowly and to tell him what certain modern words were, like ship, masts, cannons and captain.

The time went quickly and Gwyn's mam could be heard stomping up the stairs carrying the hoover. She entered the room and Egryn hid again. She turned the TV to a different channel and said that *Shaun the Sheep* was on, and he loved that programme. She said she would hoover when the programme had finished. Before she went out she told him to come down when the programme ended, as his food would be ready.

Egryn only understood bits, as his mam spoke fast, and sometimes used English words. Gwyn explained that this was the box he had told him about with moving pictures. He told Egryn to sit on his bean bag and look at the box.

When it came on, Egryn was frightened and hid behind the bag but eventually when he realized they could not come out of the so-called box, he made his way back onto the bag and watched.

It was amazing. He loved the colours especially. Egryn had seen a sheep on his travels with the outsiders and couldn't believe that these sheep could stand on two legs and speak. Also the dog walked on two legs.

Gwyn had to explain it wasn't real and it was a cartoon; Egryn didn't have a clue what a cartoon was. They were not real sheep, just ones that had been drawn. Gwyn got out a pen and drew a sheep on a piece of paper then drew some cows and horses. They watched it a bit more and Egryn laughed aloud regularly.

After it was over, when Gwyn went downstairs for his food, he decided to go back to his tree as Gwyn was popping out in the car with his mam after his meal.

On the way back to his tree, he checked the water in the trench. It was only a bit at the bottom as he had only moved the stone a little bit. He wasn't sure if he wanted to flood it now, as he was enjoying his friendship with Gwyn. So he pushed the stone back and stopped the flow. He must remember to start it again before Iori Llew came back.

CHAPTER TWENTY-NINE

AN EXCITING WEEK

The next day the arogs came early and finished the fence all the way around, and put a wicker gate in the middle opposite the front door. Egryn could either go through that, or go on one of the branches which grew over the fence and jump down. If he squeezed tightly he could just about fit through one of the gaps in the fence, but he nearly got stuck when he tried. They had also covered the back garden with artificial grass, which looked like grass but smelt different, like the one in the front.

They then got some big sections of wood and proceeded to set up a shed in the back garden. It was quite educational for Egryn to watch the construction, and he was amazed how quickly they erected it, and then left.

He was so busy watching, he never noticed Woody in the window at first, so when he made his way up the drainpipe, Gwyn asked him why he was so late.

On the TV was a nature programme about Africa and Egryn saw it. Just as he looked a crocodile walked out of the river, and Egryn ran like a bolt of lightning and got up onto the window ledge, before Gwyn shouted out, "Stop! They are not real, just pictures in the box."

Egryn hesitated, watched for a while, and eventually he realized Gwyn was correct and so made his way down.

"What's that monster called?" inquired Egryn.

Gwyn had to tell him about elephants, lions, crocodiles and tigers, etc., and explain how big and fast they were.

When the programme finished, a Tom and Jerry cartoon came on, and Egryn loved it. He kept shouting to the mouse to run faster, and got upset when Tom caught him and started bashing him. Gwyn had to explain again, it was not real. Egryn asked could they at some point get out of the box and get him, and Gwyn showed him how to press a button and turn it off.

Whenever a meal was being cooked Egryn left, as he hated the smell, especially meat. Gwyn asked why was he putting his hands over his ears and Egryn answered that it was to stop the smell. Gwyn found that odd.

One day that week he couldn't believe how bad the smell was, and had to rush out. They were having curry. He said later he could smell the stink even in his tree.

It was an educational week, as Egryn learnt all about the house, what the rooms were used for, and even got used to the horrible loud noise the vacuum cleaner made. At first he thought it was a monster.

Gwyn often sneaked up some dessert for him to try. He absolutely loved trifle, and ate every fruit-flavoured yoghurt. Any chocolate or sweets were gobbled down; he loved them all. In fact Egryn hardly ever ate any traditional elf food any more. He preferred Gwyn's. The days flew by and Egryn learnt more about the arogs' world and new words every day.

Eventually Gwyn reminded him that they were going away in the morning for seven days, and he wouldn't mind if Egryn came in through the letterbox while they were away. He warned him that once a day his uncle would be driving over to check the house so that everything must look normal, and the lights must not be put on, so that he must only come inside during the day.

What an exciting last week that was. When Gwyn's car drove away next morning, Egryn felt so miserable as he was going to miss his company so much. Yet it wasn't long ago he hated the arogs coming. Iori probably would be back today or tomorrow, in fact he was surprised he wasn't back earlier to tell him to leave. Looking at the sky and feeling the wind he knew rain was due in the next half an hour, so Iori might come soon or tomorrow when the rain had gone. He didn't have much time so he went to the stone and pushed down so it moved, and the water started trickling in the trench. He didn't want Iori to know he had moved it. Next he went up to the top of the tallest tree and looked in the direction Iori would probably be coming. But there was no sign of him.

CHAPTER THIRTY

VISITORS

The clouds were gathering and getting darker, it looked as if Iori definitely wasn't coming and Egryn was just about to climb down when he espied some movement in the hedgerow which encased the field. Looking carefully he could make out three figures coming towards him. It looked like three elves, and to his delight he recognized not just Iori, but also Alis Hâf and Rhiannon.

He rushed down the tree and when they arrived in the forest he gave them all a big hug. They all chatted excitedly at the same time and nobody understood what each of them were saying. They realized this and all stopped at the same time. The visitors gave him a visiting gift of wild strawberries and mushrooms, and they went straight away up into Brenig's tree which had more room, had a feast and told each other the news. It seemed strange to be in the king's tree without him being there.

Rhiannon had made him a new top to wear and when she gave it to him, he gave her a small item to eat. She looked at it, smelt it and nibbled a bit, then gobbled it all.

It was delicious. "What is it?" she asked.

"The arogs call it chocolate," he replied. "I kept a piece the boy arog gave me just in case I had visitors."

She passed a bit to Alis Hâf and Iori, who also loved it.

Before they did anything else, the two females decided they wanted first to go into their own family tree. As soon as they did this they breathed in, and big beaming smiles came on their faces as they sucked in the familiar scent. Every tree had its own distinctive smell and if you blindfolded an elf, they could still find their own tree easily.

They each had twenty minutes on their own, just sitting quietly in their own tree listening to the familiar rustling of the leaves. On meeting back in Brenig's tree Egryn told them that this time when they come in, it would be different as the house was now full of the arogs' furniture and clothes, etc. He told the females that if they were not sure of anything, not to touch until they'd checked with him. Also that every day an arog is coming in a zoom zoom, he didn't think he would today, but to listen out. When he did they might find a hiding spot, which he would show them. He wouldn't stay long.

They were excited and cajoled Egryn to take them now. Iori hadn't seen the fence and said, "That's new," and Egryn replied, "That's no bother, as on this side we can go through the gaps in the gate. If you follow me I will show you a spot on the fence where I have made little grooves all the way up each side. They are for emergency escapes. The grooves are there so you can put your feet in and get over even quicker."

He then reminded them of the letterbox, and how to lift it to go in and how to push it to come out. Also, again in case of emergency, to wedge it open with a little twig to make it easier. The next thing was to practise going in and out using the drainpipe and guttering, and they collected a pile of leaves and covered them with a few ferns to stop them blowing away, to have a safe landing.

"Right that's the safety sorted, now let's have a tour. Come on, Gwyn's house, here we come!"

It was funny walking on the artificial grass. Alis Hâf picked up a blade and tried to chew it. Instantly, she spat it out.

"You can't eat that," laughed Egryn. "Now listen carefully. I will show you any dangerous things not to touch and every hiding place in each room. Any questions don't be afraid to ask. Better to be safe than sorry."

They toured around for the next hour. Some of the doors were closed so the four of them had to sit on the handle and jump up and down until it flicked open. Going into Gwyn's bedroom, they noticed that Gwyn had moved the handle of the little window at the top so from the outside it looked closed but when the four of them pushed it hard, they managed to create a gap they could escape from.

Alis Hâf's favourite room was the bathroom, she loved the smells of the soaps and powders, while Rhiannon's was the lady arog's bedroom as she loved clothes. Her wardrobe had a key in it and if two of them turned it just a little, the wardrobe door opened. She loved touching the material and one silk dress was so soft that she wished she could have some material to take home with her. She couldn't take it, as an elf won't steal or take anyone else's possessions, unless they ask first.

Egryn then realized that before they went, the arogs had put their recycling bags in the shed, and Gwyn said that his uncle was coming in midweek to put them out, when he came to check. The lady arog had bought lots of new clothes to go on the holiday and Egryn remembered watching her carrying bags of old clothes to chuck out. They were in the shed, so before they went back the four of them would try to get in the shed and Rhiannon could help herself to any material she wanted.

"Great idea," she said, "that's not stealing, let's get some now." But the others said not yet, later on.

It was a lot to take in. Egryn's mouth was getting dry because he had never talked so much. He quite fancied that white stuff Gwyn called milk but he couldn't open the fridge door, not even with the four of them pulling. He had to settle for water, which you could get in the kitchen if you pulled the lever sideways.

Just as he was about to pull the lever, Iori Llew put his head close to the end of the tap to look up the hole to see what was in it. Egryn pulled and the force of water knocked Iori down into the sink. He panicked because he thought he was going down the plug hole, but just one leg did. His body jammed the hole and the water started to get deeper and would soon cover his head. He couldn't budge. Quickly the other three turned off the tap and jumped in, pulled his foot out from the hole, and thankfully the water subsided. They were all soaked, so they decided to go back to the tree as they needed new clothes, and the girls needed a bit of fresh air.

Coming out through the letterbox Rhiannon reminded them about the clothes in the shed, so Iori – he was much wetter than the others – was told to go ahead and change into some of Egryn's clothes, but not to put his new top on he had just got from Rhiannon. The other three went to the shed.

Egryn hoped Iori hadn't looked at the trench yet as he wanted it to fill up a bit more, so that they wouldn't know he had stopped the flow.

How to get in the shed might be a problem, but they were lucky the bags were stacked behind the main bin. There were three of them, one with plastic, one with paper and the third one had clothes. Now, the clothes would be too bulky and too heavy to carry back to the tree, and eventually back to Rhiannon's new house. How could they get small pieces?

"No problem!" proclaimed Rhiannon, as she put her hand inside a hidden pocket in her top, and pulled out a sharp thin piece of wood which she used as a needle and as a cutting tool.

Breaking open the thin plastic bag with the sharp needle, they pulled out a few items of clothes and Rhiannon flattened one, which she liked the colour of. Using the sharp end she created a row of little holes next to each other in the shape of a square. Now if she pulled it would tear off, which she did. Right, that was enough for today, and they put the rest back in the bag and carried the material back to the tree.

When they got back Iori was dressed in dry clothes and had a puzzled look on his brow. When the two females left to go to Rhiannon's tree to use the material, he said to Egryn, "I've seen the trench, and there doesn't seem to be as much water as there should be." Egryn just looked puzzled.

Iori looked at him and as he knew him so well, asked him, "Did you put the stone back?"

Seeing as he couldn't lie, he replied, "Yes, I did."

Iori then told Egryn that Brenig left him here to protect the trees, to stop any creature from invading their sacred forest, because the plan was eventually to come back and the flood was part of the plan. He reminded Egryn that he was to have no contact with the arogs, and they were not to know that elves exist, let alone lived next to them.

Egryn retorted, "It doesn't make any difference as it's too late, we will never come back. That little flood won't stop the arogs living in the house. They are here to stay. It's a desperate, futile attempt."

Iori thought about this before answering. He then explained that he hadn't told Brenig or anyone about Gwyn seeing him. He wasn't sure if he should. But if Brenig or anyone inquired he would have to tell the truth. The same applied to Rhiannon and Alis Hâf.

Asking him why he had really stopped the flow of water, Egryn explained that he really liked Gwyn, and was afraid that if all the trenches filled up, then the water would flow into Gwyn's garden and spoil it.

Well that was exactly what Brenig wanted, he wanted the house abandoned, and the arogs to leave forever so that they could all move back into their traditional home.

"If that happens I won't see Gwyn again."

"No, you won't. Brenig reckons that any contact with any arogs will lead to our discovery and eventually the end of our world, which has existed for over a thousand years."

"Please Iori, don't tell him I've done it and will do it again."

Egryn knew that he couldn't lie but begged him to do it. Iori said that he wouldn't lie but hoped that Brenig wouldn't ask him again, or the two girls, but he was bound to in his report this time. When he inevitably found out, he would certainly send some of the other elves to bring Egryn away and to remove the stone. He warned Egryn not to speak to Gwyn ever again or let him see him. "He cannot be your friend."

Iori said that he could stay tomorrow but had got to go back the day after to report to Brenig. When the girls came back again he told them that tomorrow would be their last day there and they must not go in the house again.

"You've had your fun, but it has to stop, contact with arogs and entering into their world is not for elves. Rhiannon, you can't take anything back with you, not even the material. We should never have gone in the house, Brenig realized this after we went in before we moved. He heard us talking and getting excited and has come to the conclusion that no contact is the best policy. I was a fool to return but Egryn, you are my best friend and I could see how excited you were to take us back again. I didn't want to disappoint you but I made a mistake.

"Girls, enjoy tomorrow relaxing back in your family tree and pretend the house isn't there. Egryn, you must do the same."

He never answered.

"Egryn, you must agree!" repeated Iori.

Egryn reluctantly nodded his head in agreement.

The next day was not the day Egryn had planned. Having glimpsed the everyday life of an arog, he wanted to find out more and he couldn't wait for Gwyn to come back. When Gwyn's uncle came to check the house, they hid in the tree but he was only there for a few minutes and then took the rubbish bags away with him. The day was long and sad and they decided to return that afternoon.

When the three were about to depart, Iori begged Egryn again not to see or speak to Gwyn. There was a good chance Brenig would send someone else in a few days to check on him, so he must be prepared to leave.

Rhiannon said that if they were allowed to come back, but she doubted they would be, she would bring him some new clothes, whilst Alis Hâf said that she would bring a selection of potions he could use if he suffered any cuts or ill effects. They gave each other especially long cwtches and hoped that Brenig would send someone else to take his place and he could come back to live with them. Egryn said that it would be nice, but he wasn't sure if he meant it.

Elves are always happy but he could feel a sadness coming over him. On the one hand he wished he had never volunteered to stay on, but on the other he was glad he had befriended Gwyn and invaded the world of the arogs. His life before the house was built seemed tame and unexciting now.

CHAPTER THIRTY-ONE

DANCING ON THE FENCE

The next day was really odd; no other elf with Egryn and Gwyn away. He had promised not to go in the house, but he didn't promise not to go in the garden. So he spent the morning on the swing and doing roly-polys on the artificial grass. The water was now filling the second trench. Should he put the stone back?

To get over the feeling of depression that was creeping up on him, he looked for something different to do. He kept seeing his friend Iori's face – would they remain friends?

He was really bored, he needed something exciting to do which he hadn't done before. So he decided to see how fast he could go around the garden racing on the top of the fence. Usually when the settlement was properly occupied there was always a lookout on top of the tallest tree, on guard duty with a carved-out ram's horn to blow to signal if any dangerous bird of prey was entering the area. Elves can see them miles off, and the warning is given in plenty of time.

As he raced on the top of the fence balancing on its narrow width, he was concentrating so hard not to fall, he failed to notice a huge bird circling in the sky. It was a red kite. There used to be thousands, but until recently they had almost died out. There hadn't been one in their area for about 20 years. But now they had multiplied and pairs were looking for new territory.

Running faster than he had for ages, he was coming towards the dodgy bit, where he had to jump down a level onto the top of the gate, then jump back up onto the fence the other side. The red kite spotted him; they can see anything moving from a long way up. He stopped circling and swooped down faster and faster. Egryn was running so fast he was breathing heavily, and this stopped him hearing the bird.

Just as he reached the gate to drop down, for his final swoop the red kite opened his jaws wide and at top speed aimed a bite at Egryn. By sheer luck he dropped down the very second the kite's jaws were about to wrap around him, and his mouth missed but his body knocked him off the fence. The bird was flying so fast it took him a few seconds to slow down and turn around. Landing on his side, Egryn realized he had just a few seconds to escape, and struggling to get up he could feel his side was wet with blood. Where could he go? He could hardly move his arm so he couldn't climb.

The bird was zooming towards him; he squeezed through a gap in the gate and it missed him. He was now inside the garden. Getting up a tree was impossible. As the bird turned and flew towards him, at the last second he decided he would have to dash and squeeze through the gap in the gate. Timing had to be just right. Getting his breath back while the bird turned around, he would then do the same thing again the other way. He did this a few times, and the bird was so close he could smell its breath and see inside its gaping mouth. The bird realized what he was doing, so decided to land. It turned and edged towards him. Looking around for somewhere safe, his only hope was the shed – the door hadn't been fitted properly and there was a gap where he might, just might, get under. What if he got stuck?

The bird strode towards him, jaws wide open. Should he try to squeeze through again knowing the bird didn't have to turn or land? He panicked and dashed for the shed, but because of his wounds wasn't as fast as normal. The bird ran towards him, and before he was halfway there it caught him, wrapped its jaws around him and opened its wings to fly up to take his victim back to his nest.

At the last second Egryn had dodged a bit, so the jaws only caught the side of his coat and he was held dangling underneath as the bird took off with just a bit of his top in his mouth. Egryn wriggled out of the coat and as the bird was only fifteen metres high so far, he fell to the ground. Because of his wound he couldn't somersault and turn to land on his feet, but landed on his back. The pain was terrible, and it knocked all the wind out of his body. It took the bird a few seconds to realize he had dropped him, and he had to do a circle to turn around and search for Egryn.

Because he landed on the artificial grass the landing wasn't as hard as on normal grass, which probably would have killed him or knocked him out. Also lying on it, it was harder for the bird to see him. Unfortunately it kept circling, getting lower and lower. It was bound to see him sooner or later.

As it passed overhead and gradually got lower and lower, he recovered his breath, and crawled a little bit towards the shed, which by sheer luck he landed a few metres from. The bird was only a few metres from the ground preparing to land close to where Egryn was laying. Egryn knew that the bird had spotted him, so he had a few seconds to spare before the bird would be on the ground right next to him. He crawled quickly and in agony to the bottom of the shed door. He squeezed under but the pain was terrible. Halfway in, he got stuck. The bird landed and bent his head to peck him, when Egryn breathed out hard and sucked his stomach in, to make himself thinner and just in time he managed to squeeze in. The bird's beak scraped his other arm just as he got through. He lay inside and could hear the bird scratching against the door and barging it. The door shook and rattled. Would it hold? It was rocking a bit more and he realized it would burst open after a few more shoves. He was soaked in blood, he could feel its wetness, as elves' blood is more like water and is almost colourless.

Next thing he heard was a zoom zoom coming. His head was spinning and he thought he heard a dog before he passed out.

He had. Gwyn's uncle had come to check, and this time brought his neighbour's dog who he had to look after while he was away. Seeing the dog, the bird flew away seconds before the door would have given way.

Time passed. Egryn was lying down. Where was he? Why was he hurting? Opening his eyes slowly he could see he was inside the shed. How was it dark? Slowly he recalled everything that had happened. He tried to move but couldn't. He was too weak to even sit up and he passed out again.

A whole day went by and he was still unconscious inside the shed.

Unknown to him, Iori Llew arrived. Unable to lie, he had told everything to Brenig, who sent him back to get Egryn to leave and report to him. He was really angry hearing that the arog boy had met Egryn, and sent Iori to be the guard in his place, reminding him not to let any of the arogs see him, unlike Egryn.

Brenig really wanted one day to come back and hoped the flooding might get the arogs to leave. However, he was sensible and clever enough to realize that it might be impossible for their existence to be a secret forever as their world, according to Selwyn's reports, was getting smaller and smaller. He was determined however to try and keep their world a secret from the arogs, for as long as possible at least.

They would probably have to go even further away from the house, find a new settlement just in case, and abandon all hopes of coming back. Their hope of using the flood would be no use if the arogs knew of their existence. He needed a proper report from Egryn about how much contact he had (if any) with any arog.

Iori stayed for a whole day and night and saw no sign of Egryn. The squirrels said they hadn't seen him for a few days. Then he discovered a red kite's feather on the grass, and picking it up felt it was damp. Smelling that spot of artificial grass he realized it was elf's blood. Knowing that the only elf in this area was Egryn, he realized the worst; his best friend had been taken by a bird. To his dismay, not far from the blood stain he could see Egryn's catapult. He knew something dreadful must have happened, as Egryn never went outside without it.

Tears flooded from his eyes, which got darker and darker. He didn't want to move from that spot, but he was worried the bird might come back, so very slowly, he reluctantly moved on.

Going to Egryn's house he took down the letter "E" which the squirrel had given him and Goronwy's walking stick. He wondered if he would ever be in this tree again.

He then went to his own tree, and sat inside for an hour. He really believed now that this was the last time he was going to be in his family home, probably for the last time ever in this wood. Brenig told him that if Egryn was not there, he was to come back to report.

Eventually he got up, sadly he gave the squirrel the news about Egryn, and headed immediately away, taking the longest route along the hedges in case the bird was still around. He wasn't going to stay as a guard as Brenig originally planned, as Egryn was supposed to report to him. The red squirrels were not just sad about Egryn, they were worried as they were now on their own. Before he went, they pleaded for Iori to come back after giving his report to Brenig, but he said that he thought they would all go on a trek to find a new bigger and safer settlement further away, and he would probably not see the red squirrels again, either.

What a sorry sight it was, the red squirrels all crying, sitting on a branch, watching Iori trudging slowly away with his head bowed, leaning on Goronwy's walking stick.

All this time Egryn was lying down in a coma, getting weaker and weaker.

CHAPTER THIRTY-TWO

IN PAIN

Not knowing how long he had been unconscious, Egryn was woken from his stupor by the sound of a car. Where was he? Oh no, he remembered. He was as weak as a kitten and in terrible pain. If only Alis Hâf was here. If he could get to his tree he could use her potions, but it was impossible.

What if someone came into the shed? They were bound to see him, as he was just inside the door. He had to move, but he couldn't. He could hardly lift his head, and felt like he was going to pass out any second.

Looking over his stomach he scanned to see where he could hide if he could move. The only place was a spade leaning by the side of the door, if he could get behind it. Trying to wriggle he moved just a few centimetres. Boy, did it hurt. Waiting for the pain to subside he tried again, moved a little bit and fainted for a short while.

In his head he could hear noises – it was the arogs unloading the car. Gracious me, a week has passed by. Will one of the adults come into the shed? If not, will he be still alive when they do? Please, let Gwyn be the first one in.

Wriggling again, he got closer to the spade. Pausing to recover, he heard Gwyn asking his dad if he could go on his bike. His dad said he could and Egryn could hear the man's footsteps coming towards the shed. Just as his hand started to open the door, his mobile phone rang and he stopped. Very lucky. He turned and walked away to speak with the caller, and just before he went into the house he told Gwyn that the door was ajar and he could get his own bike out.

Gwyn strode to the door, pulled it completely open and stepped in. His foot was just about to step on Egryn when he stopped just in time. Putting his foot aside, he stared down. He was aghast. He then moved his head closer to have a better look. Egryn muttered, "The bird…" before he fainted again.

Gwyn was in complete shock and horrified. Very gingerly, Gwyn picked him up and didn't know what to do. He turned his hand around so that he could see what wounds he had and where the blood, which had now congealed, had come from. Turning around he checked where his dad was and saw that he had gone inside the house. His mam had as well. He had a little time. Somehow he had to get him out of the shed and up to his bedroom. *Or should he just get his mam to help? Best not to*, he thought, so he put him very slowly and carefully inside the little bag he had dangling at the back of his bike. Egryn groaned in agony even though he was still unconscious.

Aware of the groans Egryn was making, Gwyn decided to sing to stop his parents hearing him. Just then his mam came out and said, "Someone's happy. I used to sing that song in school as well."

He rode around the garden, slowly waiting for the hall to be clear so he could get Egryn up the stairs. His dad came back out and walked past him to get the luggage out. At the same time he could hear his mam in the kitchen loading the washing machine.

It was now or never. He stopped the bike, got Egryn out of the bag in the palm of his hand, and walked as fast as he could up the stairs. He still had to sing as Egryn was calling out in pain. As he was just three steps up, his dad came in behind him but couldn't see Egryn.

He remarked, "Glad to be home are you?"

Luckily his dad didn't push past him and on reaching the landing, his dad went into his own bedroom with the suitcase; he had taken Gwyn's up on the previous trip. Going through his bedroom door, Gwyn kicked it shut with his foot and placed Egryn on top of the bed. *What if someone comes in? He can't stay here. Where might he be safe?* He couldn't go in a drawer as his mam often put things in it.

Seeing his toy garage in the corner, he went to a drawer, got out a thick pair of socks and made a bed at the back of the first floor, which couldn't be seen from the front. Placing Egryn gently on it he realized he had to do something. He couldn't leave him there in that pain.

What would his mam do? *Shall I ask her for help? I might have to eventually. I think she would clean his wounds first. I can't move him to the bathroom, so will have to clean him in here.* He took Egryn very carefully from the garage and lowered him slowly onto a soft jumper on the floor, by the other side of the bed which couldn't be seen if the door was opened. Good gracious, he looked so white, like a ghost.

"Please, nobody come in," he mumbled to himself. Getting a plastic container from his toy box he went to the bathroom and brought it back, full of warm, soapy water. His mam saw him from downstairs crossing on the landing, and asked, "What are you doing?"

Thinking quickly he replied, "I'm cleaning my wrestlers."

"What, all of them? You will need a much bigger bowl than that!"

"No, just the ones I took on holidays, they've got little bits of sand wedged in some of their parts."

She replied, "That was a good idea," and went back into the kitchen.

Hastily continuing into his bedroom before placing the bowl next to Egryn, he kicked the door closed with his foot.

Little by little, he peeled off Egryn's top, which was stuck to his body with dried blood. It took him ages and because Egryn moaned in pain he put on his telly to mask the noise. There was a huge gash right down his side. When he pressed the wound with a warm wet cloth, Egryn groaned louder. He cleaned it as carefully as he could. When he had a cut his mam usually put ointment on him which he knew was kept in the cupboard in the bathroom. He dashed in to get it. Squeezing the top, the cream dribbled out on his wound. Then getting a handkerchief from his drawer he wrapped it around him. He also cleaned the not-so-deep wound on his arm.

How long Egryn had been lying there in the shed, he didn't know. So he placed him on his made-up bed at the back of his toy garage and went downstairs. He told his mam he was getting some biscuits and orange juice. Instead of biscuits he got a jar of honey and taking it up with the juice, he poured a little of both into Egryn's mouth.

He kept the juice on his bedside table and hid the jar of honey in the toy box. Half an hour later he did it again. When he went to bed he thought that Egryn didn't look so white.

Gwyn couldn't sleep, so he was able to dab some honey and juice on his lips every half an hour. About 4am, Gwyn dozed off.

Waking up in the morning he checked Egryn straight away. He was breathing, still white but not so much. His eyes were closed. Dropping some juice on his lips and putting some honey on, he smiled as he could see Egryn responded and swallowed a lot more than previously. Perhaps he wouldn't have to ask his mam for help, after all.

Getting the ointment he dabbed some more on and covered it with a clean hanky, then placed a fresh sock under him. There was not much else to do. He remembered he was going to school tomorrow, so Egryn would be on his own. Also tomorrow was the day his mam always gave his bedroom a good tidy.

When he went down for breakfast, he sneaked the dirty sock and hanky into the bottom of the dirty clothes basket.

Every hour or so Gwyn popped up and dabbed Egryn's lips. About teatime Egryn opened his eyes and did not see that Gwyn was sitting on his bed, as he seemed to be inside something. Egryn tried to speak and call Gwyn's name. Luckily Gwyn was in the room, heard him and looked in the garage.

During the minute his eyes were open Gwyn explained where he was, and what treatment he had. Egryn smiled and closed his eyes again. Not long after he opened his eyes for longer, and told Gwyn to get some spider's webs and place them over his cuts, and put the ointment on top. Gwyn questioned this idea and asked Egryn whether he was sure about him doing that and Egryn replied that he was. He managed to get lots of webs from behind his drawers. Egryn wished Alis Hâf was there.

Gwyn knew that there were always webs under his bed so he managed to get some more from there and did it to both wounds. He knew it would be painful. Egryn groaned while he did it, but he knew he had to. Gwyn said that he would have to move him first thing in the morning before he went to school, otherwise his mam would be sure to find him when tidying.

He had to think. The best option was in the spare bedroom. Under the bed were a few cardboard boxes full of old photographs, which hardly anyone ever looked into, and that's what he decided to use in the morning to hide his now dear friend. Perhaps he would be rushed for time in the morning before school, so he decided that it would be better to move Egryn now. This Gwyn did, very carefully after making a soft bed inside the box with one of his jumpers.

Telling Egryn he would be back, Gwyn left after cleaning him, applying more ointment and leaving some honey on a plate next to his hand.

All the rest of the day Egryn woke for increasingly longer periods inside the cardboard box in the spare room, dipped his fingers in the saucer and licked the honey. He tried sitting up but his wound hurt and he laid back down. The day seemed very long and he thought Gwyn was gone for days.

After what seemed an eternity in which he dozed and dreamt, the day passed by, and he finally heard the spare room door open. Gwyn had his pyjamas on, gave him a great smile and put some cut-up grapes and milk on a fresh saucer. He could see that Egryn was awake for longer. Before he went to bed, Gwyn sneaked Egryn in the bathroom when he went to clean his teeth, and making sure the door was locked he put the plug in the sink and filled it with warm, soapy water.

Removing the hanky he placed Egryn carefully in the water, making sure he kept his hand underneath him, so his face wouldn't go under. He then proceeded to wash his wound, take him out and dry him. Rubbing ointment on his wound and covering it with fresh cobwebs as the water had washed the old ones away, he wrapped him in a fresh hanky. Unlocking the door and peeping out to see if it was clear, he carried Egryn back in the bedroom and placed him in the cardboard box.

Seeing as Egryn was awake for longer, he asked him details about what happened. Egryn managed to tell him, before his eyes closed and he drifted back to sleep.

CHAPTER THIRTY-THREE

THE BULLY

As the days passed Egryn got much better and could sit up. He started eating more and by Friday, Gwyn's last day in school, he was so bored and missing Gwyn's company that he decided to try and stand up. Doing so, his head spun, but he managed a few steps before tumbling back down onto his makeshift bed, inside the cardboard box. He did this a few times and got out onto the floor, doing more steps each time.

As it was the weekend Gwyn was able to spend more time in his room, especially as he couldn't go outside because it rained continuously, and moved Egryn back inside the garage. It was an opportunity for Egryn to tell Gwyn that Brenig had told him not to go in the house again, and not to see him again either. When he was well enough to leave the bedroom and go back to his own tree he would never speak to Gwyn again, and he must never tell anyone about him.

Gwyn replied, "I haven't told anyone about you, I promise, cross my heart and hope to die. You've got nothing to worry about. As for you going back to your tree and surviving on your own, it's out of the question. You are too ill to go anywhere, especially alone. It's going to be ages yet before you can move and look after yourself."

"So I'm staying, but only until I get better, then I must leave and never see you again."

"Well if you must, you must, but a lot of things can happen before you decide that. Just concentrate on getting better and do a little more each day."

During the next week whilst Gwyn was in school, every day Egryn would walk around the room, slowly at first, but as each day went on he walked further and faster. He was not sleeping in the cardboard box anymore, as he could move and hide now. He spent most of the evenings watching television with the sound off, sitting on the side of Gwyn's bean bag with him. If anyone came in, he couldn't be seen. He would look out of the window and see the trees swaying in the breeze, and longed to go out. He wondered how long before he could do so – perhaps in a few days. When Gwyn went to school on Monday, perhaps he could try and go out then.

On Friday, Gwyn came home with a worried frown and wasn't his normal, happy self. Egryn could sense there was something wrong and asked what was troubling him. Gwyn told him there was a new boy in his class who was a real bully. On the yard Gwyn spoke Welsh to his friends but this newcomer had moved into the area when his dad got a new job. Obviously he couldn't speak a word of Welsh and hated the fact that some of the children were speaking it. He was a big boy for his age and everyone in that class was scared of him.

Gwyn's friend Tomos was speaking to him in Welsh on the yard, Ryan the bully heard him, grabbed his neck from behind and squeezed it really hard, choking him. He did this to lots of children, even the girls who wouldn't go anywhere near him.

"Stop speaking that monkey language!" he demanded. "If I hear it you will get a clout around the head, or I will squeeze you until the pips come out."

Gwyn found out that he was staying in a caravan as his house wasn't ready. They all hoped that when his new house was ready, he would move schools.

That night Gwyn's dad came home from work and told him that he had good news. The man who built the house had informed him that work was starting on Monday to build two more houses, and with a bit of luck some young children might move in and be company for him.

It would be dangerous on Monday for Egryn to try and get to his own tree, as he wasn't yet as fast as he used to be, especially with all the workers arriving. So he decided to try and go on the Sunday before they came.

Unfortunately it lashed down with rain and he was bound to get soaked as he was much slower that he used to be, so he postponed his journey and concentrated on doing walks and exercises around Gwyn's bedroom.

He was getting used to eating the same as Gwyn, except for the meat. He loved a bit of a Snickers bar, as it had chocolate and nuts in it. He was drinking whatever Gwyn brought upstairs. That day he had some Coca Cola and he took a big sip from the little container Gwyn poured it into. He had never had a gassy drink before and swallowed too much. His stomach was filled with gassy bubbles and he had the loudest burp ever in his life, and sick spewed out of his mouth all over Gwyn's shoes.

"Serves you right, don't swig so much, just little sips next time, and I bet you will love it. Nibble this biscuit, it will take the sick taste away."

Gwyn gave him a piece of a chocolate digestive, and he munched away happily, forgetting about being sick.

CHAPTER THIRTY-FOUR

MOVING BACK

Monday came and Gwyn pretended that he didn't want to go to school as he had a sore throat. His mam believed him as he was never ill, and Gwyn spent most of the day peering out of his bedroom window with Egryn, watching the workmen arrive.

On discovering the water-filled trenches they used the big digger and inserted a huge new drainpipe to take the water from the other side of the pond and connect it to a new ditch, which made it run downhill eventually joining another stream. All Morris's work was now of no use, and the flooding would not now interfere with the building of the two new houses. This time there were a lot more men working and it looked like the two houses would be built much quicker than the first one.

After two days pretending to be ill, his mam decided he was well enough to go to school.

When he came home that night he told Egryn that Ryan, the bully, was still there and was even worse. If anyone on the yard had sweets or chocolate he would twist their arm until they gave them to him. It really hurt. Ryan warned them that if they spoke even one word to the teacher about him, he would stick their head down the toilet and flush it.

Gwyn was not happy at all and told his mam he was too ill to go in the morning. She told him not to be a baby bunting and go.

"Your *Tadcu* [grandfather] went to your school until he was eleven and never missed a day. You are going, and I don't want to hear any more about it."

Egryn decided it was time for him to get back to his tree, and he would try and make a new catapult so that Gwyn could use it to fire at the bully. Gwyn said that he would not be allowed to take it to school.

Egryn came up with a good idea. He knew of a plant that grew near his tree, which Alis Hâf told him about. If you ground it into a powder, Gwyn could put it into the bully's clothes or shoes.

"A great idea," replied Gwyn, as they took in special clothes and footwear for *ymarfer corff* (physical education) twice a week. "What does it do?"

"Wait and see. It should work."

So that night after the workmen had gone, Egryn decided to get to his new tree carrying enough food to last him a few days: chocolate, grapes, a carrot and a bit of a banana.

He waited until it was getting dark as he would be slower than normal and there was less chance of Gwyn's parents seeing him crossing the artificial grass. Sliding down the pole would cause him some pain, so Gwyn said he was going out on his swing and carried Egryn inside his jacket.

Sitting on it with his back to the house, he released Egryn who crawled to the gate and sneaked through it, and was gone. It took him ages to get to his tree and he struggled to get up it, but eventually managed and immediately fell into a sleep trance as he was exhausted.

It was the best sleep he'd had for ages. How he missed the swishing sound of the leaves. There really is nothing like sleeping in your own home.

He slept right through to the morning, much later than normal, and was awoken by the workmen arriving. When he got up he put on some new clothes, as the old ones were all ripped and tattered. If only Rhiannon was here, she would repair them or make him some new ones.

Nibbling some chocolate for energy, he made his way stiffly to a spot where he could see the progress made on the two houses and was shocked to see how much the work had advanced already. He now realized they could never all settle back here again. Their settlement was destroyed forever and there was now no clearing, even more trees had gone, including a few oak ones. All hopes of a return had been dashed.

Egryn wondered if Brenig would have sent another elf, probably Selwyn, to check on the settlement and if so, had he reported all these new buildings going up? If he had, Brenig would surely then realize they could never come back and would make a more intense search for a new settlement further away. Egryn realized then, that he might never see his clan again.

The pond was covered over and drained and also lots of the fruit bushes had been dug up. More trees cut down or trimmed. What a terrible sight.

There was no chance of him getting the itching powder until the workmen had gone. He saw Gwyn getting in the car with his school uniform on and he was obviously looking around to see if he could spot him.

By travelling along the branches, he managed to get to the other side of the wood to the squirrel's tree and they were shocked to see he was alive. They remarked that he was much thinner and whiter and didn't appear to be moving so effortlessly.

He told them all about his attack and showed them his wounds. They asked how he had survived and he recalled all the help he'd had from Gwyn. The squirrels were surprised to hear that an arog had been so friendly and said perhaps they were not the monsters they thought they were.

Seymour then remembered that he hadn't told him about Iori's visit. On hearing his friend's name, Egryn was saddened as he missed him so much and realized he might never see him again. Especially as Iori had told Seymour of problems they were having in the new settlement, and that they might have to move further away. Seymour said that now that they thought Egryn was dead there wasn't much chance of them coming back – even if they did, when they saw the new buildings a move here would be out of the question. The squirrels confirmed that Selwyn had visited as well, as Brenig wanted a second opinion.

That morning Egryn noticed Goronwy's stick had gone and so had the letter sign on his wall Seymour had given him. He knew that Iori must have taken them, thinking he was dead.

Seymour reported that a grey squirrel had been seen spying on them for a few days, checking to see if the elves had really left, and they were worried that they would be attacked again soon. Egryn's top priority was to make a new catapult, but he doubted if he alone could stop a big attack, especially now he wasn't so strong or mobile.

Going back to his own tree for a rest, as he was still not completely back to normal, he went on a little expedition to the side of the woods furthest from the workmen. Whilst looking for a new piece of wood for his catapult, he gathered some plants to grind into the itching powder.

The plants were low on the ground and just as he gathered some, he could smell smoke. One thing elves hate is fire. His first instinct was to get up high, and he then made his way in the direction of the smoke. As he got nearer the smoke got thicker and he could hear branches starting to crackle, the noise getting louder and louder. To his utter dismay he could see a huge bonfire and branches he once knew were now burning, while an arog was dragging others and putting them on top of the flames.

It was one of the saddest sights he had ever seen. He recognized the branches the arog was dragging now, as they were from the terrible twins' tree. Many a time he had walked along them. He had to move as the smoke was making him cough and he couldn't stand watching any more.

On the way back he spotted a great piece of wood for a catapult, but wondered how he was going to get it. In the past, if you wanted a piece cut it had to be done by Selwyn, who was the only elf allowed to have a weapon made out of what the arogs called metal. Perhaps if he went to Selwyn's tree he might find some that he had cut ready to be made.

First of all he used two stones to grind the cuttings into an itching powder, which he wrapped into a big leaf ready to give to Gwyn. Then after resting again he went to Selwyn's tree, being careful as he could now be seen from the houses, the three trees in front of it were chopped down, none of them oaks, luckily. Searching for ages, he was just about to leave when he espied a piece of wood jammed into a hole inside the trunk. Perfect. Selwyn must have missed this one.

Pulling it out, he could see that it was shaped ready for a catapult. Now, about 20 years ago Selwyn's father had brought back some stretching material which the arogs called a rubber sheet. When an elf was born, they were given a half a metre long thin strip which he cut from it, and it could be used for about three perhaps four catapults. This was to last you all your life, so you looked after it. Egryn had only used one strip, so he had everything he needed to make a new one.

What a busy day. When Gwyn got home he was starving as young boys always are, but even more so today as Ryan had taken his crisps and chocolate biscuit out of his lunch box.

Waiting for the arogs to leave, Egryn made his way to the house with the itching powder. He was still too weak to climb up the drainpipe, so he waited until Gwyn's mam came out to peg clothes on the line, then he went in through the open back door. If the kitchen door was closed he might have to come back out again. It was a bit risky, but it usually took his mam quite a few minutes to peg out the clothes.

The door was open, and shooting out he struggled up the stairs and eventually got to Gwyn's bedroom, where the door was always left open. He was not there, so Egryn hid under the bed and rested, waiting for him.

After about a half an hour he could hear him coming up and as usual Gwyn gave Egryn a big smile when he saw him. They gave each other the news, and Egryn explained to Gwyn how to use the itching powder. Gwyn couldn't wait until the morning as he had *ymarfer corff* that day.

It was difficult getting around while so many workmen were moving back and forth, and so many lorries were coming and going. Some stone chippings had been tipped onto the lane to make it easier for the lorries. Egryn put his foot on a bit and found it hard to walk on, as there were lots of sharp bits sticking up.

Egryn told Gwyn which tree he would be in, Gwyn looked in that direction and waved as he was getting in the car. Most of the day was spent making his catapult and some new clothes, which he was not very good at as Rhiannon usually made them for him.

He found it really noisy now with all the machines going, lorries arriving, items getting dumped, two music machines blaring. He now realized how good what Gwyn called "double glazing" was at keeping out the noise. The air was often dusty, so he hardly went out. He couldn't wait to hear if Gwyn had used the itching powder, and if he did, what had happened.

CHAPTER THIRTY-FIVE

ACCIDENTS IN SCHOOL

He was excited when Gwyn came home and saw the signal in the window, and decided he was fit enough to get up the pipe, which he managed, but it was a struggle.

Before he even got his breath back he blurted out, "Gwynnie, come on, tell me, did it work. What happened?"

Gwyn told him that just before they had *ymarfer corff* he asked the teacher if he could go to the toilet. Passing through the cloakroom, he could see Ryan's bag containing his kit, and he sprinkled some powder in his shorts, top and trainers. Egryn had told him how much to sprinkle, and said that it takes about five minutes to work.

The lesson started, they got changed, and Gwyn was the slowest doing it, deliberately, so he was the last and only one in the changing room. This gave him time to sprinkle some on Ryan's ordinary clothes.

After a few minutes he could see Ryan having the odd scratch, and he gradually did it more and more. Eventually he was lying on his back, scratching every part of his body non-stop and shouting out, "Help! Help! I'm being attacked by an itching monster!"

The teacher had to stop the lesson, and before sending for a male teacher to come and get Ryan and take him in the showers, she had to ask the class to stop laughing. That took a while before the teacher came, and Ryan was scratching so much his nails were breaking his skin, and blood spots were breaking through. He was crying in agony when he went out. Nobody had any sympathy. They all looked at each other, smirking.

At the end of the lesson they all changed and went back to their classroom. After about ten minutes Ryan came in rather sheepish with a red face. No sooner had he sat down he started scratching again. Within minutes he started shouting out "Oh no, not again. Help! Help! Blinking heck, get them off!"

The teacher reprimanded him for swearing, saying, "I know you are in discomfort, but using bad language won't help."

"Well get the blighters off me then!"

Hearing this, the class gasped out loud and Mrs Jones shouted out, "That's enough, Ryan, I won't have language like that spoken in my class!"

"Well stop it, you silly cow!"

"That's it, Gwilym, go and get Mr Evans, please, ask him to come back again!"

He came quite quickly. The whole episode was repeated and he had his second shower of the day. This time when he came back in, he was wearing ill-fitting clothes which were too small for him, as he was big for his age. They were the only spare ones they had. He looked so comical. They were dying to laugh, though a bit scared, but after one pupil burst out loud the others all did the same. The teacher had to tell the class to stop laughing, although she found it difficult not to as well.

Ryan wasn't scratching any more but Mr Evans must have rubbed some ointment all over him as the class could all smell it. Ryan never spoke again all day and didn't go out for play in the afternoon. Gwyn thanked Egryn for a brilliant idea and hoped Ryan had learnt his lesson.

For the next few days Ryan was quiet, but then when Gwyn went to the toilet Ryan followed him in, and grabbed him from behind around the neck and screamed.

"It was you, wasn't it? You put something on my clothes." Gwyn could hardly answer as he was being choked.

"It must be you as you were the only one who went out to the toilet. Admit it."

Gwyn was tougher than he looked, and realized if he said yes Ryan would do something really horrible to him, but if he denied it, he wouldn't be sure and would not hurt him so much. He managed to blurt out that it wasn't him, but Ryan didn't believe him, hauled him to the toilet and shoved his head down in the water, and brought it back up again.

"It was you, admit it!"

He didn't, but he couldn't anyway as his mouth was full of horrible toilet water. His head was shoved down again and this time Ryan kept holding it down and flushed it.

He thought he was going to drown or choke, but when his head was pulled back up he still denied it.

"Right perhaps it wasn't you then, but I will find out who it was, and that person will have their head shoved down one with poo in it. If no one confesses I will do it to all the boys and the girls. Now get lost!"

Charming! He let Gwyn go and did it to two of the boys he suspected during the lunch break. In the afternoon break he came out of the class behind Osian. Poor Osian was so scared he said he had done it, hoping not to have his head ducked.

What a mistake. He shouldn't have. Ryan dragged him to another cubicle where he had just had a big poo at the end of lunch break and hadn't flushed it. He shoved Osian's head in very roughly for ten seconds, three times.

He warned him if he told the teacher he would have it ten times next time, for longer as well. So Osian, crying his eyes out, was so terrified he peed himself, and the others helped him to clean up, and were asked not to tell the teacher.

When Egryn heard this, he knew exactly what he could do next. This couldn't go on. He knew of a concoction of plants and flowers which would make you go to the toilet for a wee every 20 minutes, with no warning. Alis Hâf had told him about it. Once Morgan and Meredydd had eaten the wrong mushrooms, and were in agony with severe stomach pains. After they drank the mixed-up potion, they peed every 20 minutes for a few hours and the stomach pain finally went away. They were cured. Problem was how to get Ryan to eat it, as it would be easier to mask its taste in food than a drink.

They knew he was a greedy guts. When it was a child's birthday it was customary to take a cake in for the whole class to have a slice. Egryn remembered you only needed a teaspoon of the powder for it to work.

The next birthday was in two days and it was Mali's, who hated Ryan. So Gwyn gave her some powder, and told her to ask her mam to cut the cake into slices. Knowing how greedy Ryan was, she put the powder in the biggest slice.

When breaktime came the teacher told the children to line up and Mali would give each one a piece on the way out. Being careful not to give the first ones the big slice, she then saw Ryan pushing himself to the front. She picked up the smallest piece and held it out for Ryan to have.

"I don't want that one, this bit is mine!" he announced and grabbed the biggest piece as she expected. He virtually gobbled it down before he got out the door.

About ten minutes later he was wandering around the yard on his own, as nobody would play with him, looking for anyone who might have sweets. Suddenly he stopped, looked down and could see a puddle forming between his legs.

One of the older boys pointed to him and shouted, "Look, Ryan has peed himself!"

Everyone gathered around, and once one child laughed they all did. Ryan was led inside and given clothes from the emergency bag to wear again, and he looked really comical coming into the classroom after play had finished, wearing clothes that were obviously not his.

Ten minutes later Ryan cried out as another puddle formed under his seat in the class. The whole event was repeated. In front of everyone, Ryan again came back in clothes far too small for him. He was really embarrassed and kept his head bowed down, ashamed to look at the class's smiling, staring faces.

He was told that if he felt like he wanted to go, not to ask, but to go straight out. It was no good, it happened a third time and they had to phone his dad to come and get him.

The children in the class could see Ryan's father through the window, dragging him across the yard by his ear and before he shoved him in the boot, he gave him a nasty clip around the head.

Ryan blurted out that he wanted to go in the car but his father told him that no baby bunting who wets his pants was going to stink his car out, and he shoved his head down as he slammed the lid of the boot closed, just missing his head.

Egryn really enjoyed hearing about Ryan's problems.

"Well it was nice to hear about a bully being bullied."

"Yes it was, that was a brilliant idea, Egryn, I never thought it would work out as well as it did."

With that he put his hand up to a shelf and hid something behind his back.

"Surprise, surprise, guess what it is."

Egryn made a few guesses to no avail. "Enough guesses, come on, show me!"

He had brought up a packet of honey glazed nuts which his mam had bought in Sainsburys. He hid them on the shelf. Egryn loved them, and Gwyn remembered this. By now Egryn preferred the goodies Gwyn kept giving him to the natural food he had eaten all his life. Gwyn remembered how last time he enjoyed listening to Egryn muttering groans of delight as he licked the honey off before nibbling the rest of the nut.

Gwyn brought his hands out from his back and shouted out, "Whallah!"

He then ripped the packet open and for the next half an hour, watched Egryn licking and munching away and purring in great delight.

CHAPTER THIRTY-SIX

THE ATTACK

On Saturday Gwyn as usual could spend a lot more time with Egryn, and they were in the bedroom when Gwyn saw a car he hadn't seen before pull up. Two men and a woman got out, and were looking at the almost finished house next door. One of the men unlocked the door, and the three went inside.

Egryn turned when Gwyn shouted out, "Oh no. It can't be. Please don't let it be."

"What's the matter?" asked Egryn.

"I can't believe my eyes!"

"Believe what!"

"I hope I've made a mistake, but I've seen one of those men before."

"Where! Who is it?"

"The first man who came out, remember I only saw him for a little bit before he went in, looks exactly like the same man who picked Ryan up from school."

"You mean his horrible, nasty father?"

"I do. Let's hope I'm wrong."

171

"If it is, what is he doing here?"

"Well, it might be his father perhaps. Ryan did say when he arrived they were moving into a new house, but I never imagined it would be next to me."

They never moved and kept staring at the house next door. Eventually they came out.

"Oh my God, it's him, definitely."

"Are you sure?"

"Yes, I recognized his ugly chops. Not many people have got an angry face like that."

"What's chops?"

"It's another name for someone's face. Anyway, visiting a house doesn't mean they are buying it. My parents looked at loads before they decided on this one. Come on, let's watch telly. It will take our mind off things."

That night, like almost every other night, Gwyn watched his favourite TV programmes and Egryn watched with him. Gwyn usually sat on his bean bag and Egryn sat on the side, away from the door so that he couldn't be seen if anyone came in. If they did he could scurry back under the bed. He got to love it, especially if Gwyn had crisps, sweets or chocolate. He realized now they were not real, just moving pictures, and they couldn't come out of the screen.

He especially liked the Toy Story films. He recognized Buzz Lightyear, and remembered when he pressed the button and thought he was real. Gwyn played him some scenes from *Lord of the Rings*, where Legolas the elf appears. Egryn exclaimed that he was too tall and nothing like real elves. He especially liked Mallificent and loved seeing her zooming across the sky and repairing broken tree branches.

On weekday nights and weekends, he spent hardly any time in his own tree, and tended to only go there to sleep.

The next Monday, when Gwyn was in school, he went to see Seymour and had a shock when he found the tree deserted. Not a red squirrel in sight. All the stored nuts were gone. He couldn't remember this tree ever existing without a red squirrel, and his grandfather told him they were there when he was little.

He came back a different way to his own tree and saw on the ground Solomon, Seymour's grandfather, lying on his back. Rushing towards him he could see he was still breathing, but only just. There were bite marks on his body, and when he struggled to speak some blood escaped from his mouth. Somehow he managed to speak a few words at a time, and Egryn heard how they were attacked by the grey squirrels and had to escape out of the forest. Because he was old, he was much slower, and they caught him and clawed and bit him.

He asked Egryn where he had been when they needed him, but he was too ashamed to say watching television in Gwyn's bedroom. Suddenly Solomon appeared to choke, and his mouth opened, a large gushing of blood escaped and his eyes remained open staring at the sky. He had breathed his last.

Staring at his lifeless body and feeling guilty at not being here to help him, Egryn saw just in time a shadow flying towards him, and at the last second he dashed sideways behind a tree, and a red kite swooped past. He had obviously spied the squirrel's body from above.

He knew every branch of every tree in that woods, especially now as many of the trees had gone, and so he climbed up an ash tree which was next to the tree he was hiding behind. It had a hole in its trunk which he knew he could squeeze into. This he did, and after watching the red kite land, tear a piece of Solomon off with his sharp beak and talons and fly away, he made his way sadly to his own tree.

That was the first night for a long time he didn't go to see Gwyn. He felt so guilty as he had never seen anyone killed before. Suddenly the woods seemed empty and even quieter, and definitely nastier.

Gwyn kept going to the window to look for him as he missed him so much, and when it got dark he realized he wasn't coming so went downstairs.

His dad said that it was nice to see him as he spent too much time stuck in that bedroom on his own. For the rest of that evening, Gwyn showed his dad his favourite wrestlers and played a game of pairs with his wrestler cards.

His dad usually let him win most games they played, but Gwyn won easily even though his dad tried his best.

Meanwhile Egryn was sitting quite still, realizing that except for Gwyn, he now had nobody. Should he leave and go to the new settlement? If he did they would realize he was still alive, and would know when they heard about the new houses being built and more trees destroyed that there was now no chance of them settling back here. He was stuck between two completely different worlds. He loved his exciting times with Gwyn, in his world, but realized it was impossible for him to live in both worlds.

Iori had told Seymour that the new settlements were not as good as they thought, and they couldn't all be together.

So there was a big possibility that they would have moved further away. He might never find them, or he might get killed searching. Perhaps before moving they might come back and check this settlement.

He started speaking to himself. He did this far more than he used to.

"Yes, that's what I will do, I will carry on seeing Gwyn and living in his own world for the next week. Then, if I get a visit, I will decide whether to stay or move back with them. Iori's bound to come to check on me. I bet Rhiannon and Alis Hâf are missing me. Perhaps they will come as well."

He then put seven acorns lined with honey in a row along a groove inside his tree. He made the decision to eat one first thing every morning and when they were all gone, would consider whether to leave or stay.

CHAPTER THIRTY-SEVEN

MCDONALD'S

The next day he visited Gwyn after school and told him about Solomon. To try to cheer him up, Gwyn explained that from now on his mam was going to choir practice on Tuesdays and Thursdays. His mam had been in the choir before but gave up when Gwyn was born. So on those days, his dad would make tea and tonight he was bringing home a McDonald's meal for Gwyn, to save cooking. His dad hated cooking, and was useless. Last time he let Gwyn pick. He had chips and a choc ice on the same plate and was told not to tell his mam.

For dessert tonight, he was having a McFlurry ice cream with Smarties on top. "You will love it," Gwyn told Egryn, who asked how he would get it home without it melting, and Gwyn replied that his dad had got a little ice box which would keep the ice cream cold, whilst the Big Mac and chips could be warmed in the microwave.

When his dad got home his mam immediately went out, and he called Gwyn to come down as he warmed his meal in the microwave. After eating it downstairs with his dad he came up with the McFlurry and Egryn loved it, especially the Smarties on the top. He was getting used to the cooking smells now, and Gwyn asked him to try a bit of his burger next time. He knew Egryn loved tomato ketchup now so he asked his dad next time to bring a few sachets.

When his mam came home, she was singing as she came through the door and was as happy as Larry. She told his dad, Gwyn was in bed, that re-joining was the best thing she had done and was so glad to see her friends again. In fact she had invited her friend Siân to come over on Saturday and she would be bringing her son Aled, as he was the same age as Gwyn. It would be good company for him.

Egryn was getting used to spending hours indoors with Gwyn now, and didn't find it quite so stuffy. Gwyn suggested he slept in the house to save going back and forth, and he could see him in the morning before he went to school. Perhaps he could try on Thursday when his mam would be out again and he could have some McDonald's food for supper.

Gwyn seemed happier in school now. He wasn't being bullied as much, as Ryan was still embarrassed about his accidents, but he still looked forward to half term when he would be home with Egryn all day.

Thursday came, and this time Gwyn came upstairs with a bit of his burger left, and squeezed a sachet of tomato ketchup over it and told Egryn to have a bite. It was OK as it wasn't real meat, it was a vegetarian burger. So Egryn nibbled away and chewed it for a bit, swished it around his mouth then swallowed.

Stating that it was quite tasty, he bit another bit. Gwyn had fibbed, it was a real meat one, but he decided not to tell him. He then went down and came up with a strawberry sundae. Egryn's eyes nearly popped out of his head, and he devoured his bit and said that was the nicest thing he had ever tasted.

"If you think that was nice wait until next time, as I will ask my dad to bring a different one every week. It would have to be on a Tuesday only, as my mam said it's not good having two a week. On Thursdays my dad will have to cook, I bet it will be sausages, chips and beans, that's all he can do reasonably well. He had a row off my mam the other night as she asked what I would really like, and I said a choc ice and chips again. 'For goodness' sake, Huw, that's not a healthy meal for a boy to eat. Don't give him that again,' she said."

That night, a bed was prepared for Egryn on top of Gwyn's wardrobe. He made sure he dusted it first, which he could do if he stood on the bed. Egryn looked at it, then looked at the rain belting down outside. He decided to stay. This would be the first time an elf had slept inside an arog's house all night, not counting the time he was ill.

When the curtains were drawn and the light put out it was completely dark. Elves usually slept or went into their sleep trance outside for about half of the year, according to the weather. They loved looking at the stars, and it took Egryn a while to get into a trance as he could hear Gwyn breathing, and it was too hot and stuffy.

It was strange being with Gwyn before he went to school, and he watched, peeping from the edge of the top of the wardrobe, as Gwyn got dressed and rushed about, and eventually dashed downstairs to gulp his breakfast before he went to school.

Gwyn's mam went out later on, riding her bike. She had a little basket on the front and often came back with it full of items she had purchased. It was funny to be in the house on his own. He didn't really like it, so made his way out to his tree, before the workmen arrived.

As he didn't see Gwyn much in the morning before he went to school he decided to sleep in his tree on schooldays and perhaps try sleeping in Gwyn's room in the house on Saturday.

CHAPTER THIRTY-EIGHT

FOOTBALL AND MINI RUGBY

The two houses looked almost finished, and the number of workmen was getting less. Gwyn's dad said that he thought the houses would be occupied in two weeks at the most.

When his mam went out on Thursday his dad this time brought home a pizza, as he didn't want to cook sausages. Gwyn just liked the basic ones like margheritas, whilst his dad liked double pepperoni and peppers. Eating most of it downstairs, Gwyn took a small piece up for Egryn. He knew he liked cheese so he swallowed a very small piece of margherita and wanted a bit more, so Gwyn broke off a small piece of the pepperoni one and pushed it in Egryn's mouth before he could smell it. He jumped up and shouted, "My tongue is on fire!"

He ran out of the door without checking and into the bathroom to get a drink, but he couldn't turn the tap. Gwyn ran after him laughing and turned it on for him. He apologized and showed him the two different pieces, and Egryn smelt them and declared he would stick to the margherita from now on.

On Saturday the visitors came and Gwyn showed Aled his bedroom, his toys and the swing in the garden. He wanted him to see Egryn but realized he had better not, as he had promised to keep him a secret.

Egryn was left on his own and watched them from his tree, as they were playing football in the garden. They appeared to get on very well and enjoyed each other's company. Aled told Gwyn he was quite good and said he should join his teams. He played football on Saturday morning and mini rugby on Sunday morning.

Siân said it would be company for Aled and she could pick Gwyn up on Saturday at 9am to see if he liked it.

"Yes please," begged Gwyn and his mam replied, "Why not? Be good for him to get out more. He's got no company out here in this house on its own."

On Friday after school, Egryn didn't see Gwyn as his dad, had taken him to a sports shop to buy some kit after work.

Egryn's favourite day was Saturday as he usually had company most of the day and he looked forward to it, but this week he was saddened to see Gwyn go off in a car with Siân.

Even worse, a few minutes later a furniture van arrived as someone was moving into the house next door. Behind the van, to his horror, was a car and two adults, a boy and a massive dog got out. The dog wasn't on a lead and was running around the garden barking furiously. The man kept shouting for the dog to shut up but he was so excited in his new surroundings that he didn't.

The result was the man kicked the dog nastily on the bum, tied a lead on him and wrapped the lead around a drainpipe. For a few hours workmen carried items into the house, and one of them was a big wooden kennel which was deposited in the garden, and the dog was tied to that.

Quite late in the day Gwyn came back as he had gone after football to Aled's house for dinner and had stayed a few hours. He had a shock seeing the house next door occupied, and an even greater shock when he recognized Ryan's dad's car.

He still hoped that it wasn't his car but he didn't have much chance to find out as it rained for the rest of the day and nobody came out of that house. Siân came again and took him off to mini rugby on Sunday, leaving Egryn on his own once more.

Quite late in the morning the boy, who he now realized was Ryan, came out and teased the dog by throwing stones at him. He couldn't run away because of the lead. He got fed up with this, went back in the house and came out with a knife. He walked to the nearest tree, pulled down a branch and started cutting it off. He then made what he called a spear and threw it at any bird that happened to come into the garden.

His dad came out with cardboard boxes of rubbish and emptied them in a pile. He then poured some petrol on it and set fire to it. Black smoke billowed out and Egryn had to move to try to avoid it. Mrs Rees, Gwyn's mam, came rushing out to gather clothes drying on the line. After taking them in, she went over to the fence and asked Ryan's dad if he knew that the area was a smokeless zone and fires were not allowed.

"I couldn't care less," he rudely replied, "who's going to report me, YOU?" and he glared nastily at her.

Not a great start to the relationship with her new neighbour. She thought Egryn wasn't happy either as elves hate fires.

Next thing he knew Ryan's dad untied the dog and walked out of the gate with him. Having no lead, he ran furiously round each tree and peed on the trunk of three of them. Standing on two feet and scrambling furiously with his claws, he scratched the bark on Egryn's tree and barked loudly whilst looking up, forcing Egryn to go inside the little hole in the trunk. He was shaking like a leaf hoping the dog couldn't climb.

After a while the barking stopped and Egryn decided to stay inside for safety. But the wind changed directions and the smoke was now passing through the branches of his tree. He had to come out to see. Checking to see if the fire had spread, he peeped out, coughed like mad, and went back in.

All in all it was a boring day, Gwyn wasn't home till late and forgot to put Woody in the window, so Egryn spent the whole day on his own, scared stiff and stuck in the tree.

When his mam described the family next door Gwyn realized it definitely was Ryan, and didn't want to go out in the garden in case he saw him.

Egryn thought this was probably the most boring weekend he had ever had, on his own all the time.

CHAPTER THIRTY-NINE

VISITORS

As Gwyn was back in school, Egryn was alone again on Monday for most of the day. He didn't even have the red squirrels to talk to now. Still, he went to check their tree and everything had gone from it, no food stored anywhere, and no sign of the grey ones coming to live in it.

What he noticed was Ryan's house hadn't been given their refuse bin yet, so what they were doing was throwing their waste outside their garden behind one of the trees. This included leftover food which began to rot and smell. Also, during the day the gate of their garden was left open, and the dog was allowed to wander for hours not on a lead. It was getting impossible for Egryn to move around on the floor.

When Gwyn came home he would have his tea, then his mam made him do his homework, which he hated doing, so it wasn't until about six o'clock that Egryn could go and see him. Still he had to be careful, making sure Gwyn's gate was closed before he ventured onto the ground, or next door's dog would get in and it would be nearly impossible to cross the garden to get in the house.

For the first half an hour, all Gwyn talked about was what he and Aled had done in school. He didn't seem to be interested in what Egryn had done. Then most nights he told Egryn that he was going in the garden to play ball, as he needed to practice now he was in a team. All Egryn could do was watch from a tree on the furthest side. He couldn't risk being flattened by a ball, and if he went in a tree near Ryan's house the dog just barked non-stop at him. His horrible owner might come out and wonder what he was barking at, and even bring his gun, which Gwyn told him he had. He didn't fancy being shot at.

It didn't take long before Gwyn kicked the ball accidentally over the fence. No sooner had it landed than Ryan's dad, Karl, shot it. He had been waiting for the chance, as he had been staring from his bedroom window.

Gwyn ran in crying, and his mam rushed out and shouted at Karl in the window.

"Why did you have to do that? I'm going to get the police on you!"

"Go on then, but if you do then you will need four new tyres," and to justify his threat, he shot and the bullet churned up the grass just in front of their car's front tyre.

"Ha, ha, ha, there's lots more bullets where that came from. Now get in you interfering old busybody before I cop you one on your bum."

His mam ran in scared stiff, and told Gwyn to play in the house from now on.

For the first time since he met Gwyn he felt alone, and his days were quite empty and long. He even wished the house had never been built and things were like they were before the arogs came. He didn't fancy crossing the garden in case Karl was still in the window. Even worse, Ryan came out with a shovel and started digging a hole with a spade. No sooner had he started than his dad rushed out and shouted, "You stupid knucklehead, don't bury those rats in the garden, do it in the woods! Out there NOW!"

The next morning Egryn watched Gwyn going off to school, listened to the dog barking at him as he moved from tree to tree, and wondered what he would do all day again on his own. Tonight Gwyn was off to football practice. It was a good chance for him to go out to the back edge of the forest to get blackberries, as his stock was getting low. He couldn't just eat Gwyn's food all the time, especially now that he was not seeing him so much. Checking that the dog's gate was closed, he travelled from branch to branch and alighted on the grass just in front of a huge pile of blackberry bushes.

Stuffing them in his mouth first, then wrapping some in some big leaves to take back he thought he could hear something moving towards him. Concealing himself inside the brambles, he waited and watched. About a minute later who should be coming along but Iwan and Gruffydd, the wild elves. They said they might be back some time. Emerging from behind the blackberry bushes, he made them jump up in fright, and Iwan drew a metal dagger and pointed it at Egryn, but realized it was him just in time and lowered it.

They couldn't believe it was Egryn. They asked him if he was a ghost as Iori Llew had told them he was dead.

"I obviously am not!" he replied.

Egryn asked him what it was in his hand, as elves were not allowed weapons and Iwan told him it was a dagger. He pinched it from the arogs, as it was a dangerous time and things were not like they used to be. Gruffydd pulled one out and showed his as well. Egryn asked him what pinching was, and Gruffydd said, "It's stealing really."

"That's a terrible thing to do, elves are not supposed to steal. That's really bad."

They answered that they lived in the wild now, times were changing, it was really dangerous, and if he lived like them he would do the same.

Egryn then told them that they had to move, for it was dangerous to stay on the ground, as the gate might be opened and the dog would come. So he jumped up onto the lowest branch, told them to follow him and off he went to his tree.

They were shocked to see the houses, and many of the trees gone as well as the pond. This place had changed and not for the better. Egryn described his new neighbours. Hearing all this and the fact that red squirrels didn't live here any more, they told Egryn he would be better off if he came wandering with them.

"There's nothing here for you now but danger."

Egryn explained that tomorrow morning when the seventh acorn would be eaten, he was going to decide whether to stay or leave anyway.

Egryn asked them where they had seen Iori Llew. They told him that since Selwyn's injury, Iori Llew had taken over his role and was now the spy. They had bumped into him when passing near their new camp, and he told them about Egryn being killed by a bird, probably by a red kite according to the feathers. He was still upset about it, and also the fact that their new settlements were being encroached by humans. A mountain bike trail was passing through their trees in the new settlement nearby and they would most probably have to move again.

Even worse news was that between the main road and this forest, a new housing development consisting of at least 30 buildings had been started. This would mean that arogs were bound to come into this area, as it was going to be made into a nature trail, with benches and cycle tracks.

Just then they were interrupted by a dog barking at the foot of the tree. Instantly Gruffydd went out of the hole and shot his catapult at the dog, who gave a pained growl and stormed off. They inquired where the dog came from and Egryn led them to a branch in a tree where they could see the gardens and showed them the open gate.

Whilst looking, they smelt the rubbish that had been dumped, and even worse could see rats burrowing in and out of it.

"That's no good, once you have one rat, in a short while you could have hundreds. Seeing these is really bad news." So the three of them aimed their catapults at any rat that showed its face out of the pile of rubbish. All they did was force them to go back inside the dump.

They told Egryn that this was a huge problem because as long as there was rubbish dumped, the rats will come. It was really dangerous for him as it wouldn't be long until one of them smelt his scent and discovered where he lived. The only thing he could do was rub his body with something like honeysuckle every day to mask his scent. It would probably work but he must still be careful.

Both said they didn't like this place anymore and would be off that very night. If Egryn wanted they would call in and tell Iori Llew, if they could find him, that he was still alive and he would probably come to visit him if he hadn't moved further away already. Egryn said he would like that.

They asked him if he wanted to come with them and live the life of a wild elf. Egryn looked at them with their hair dangling down, tied in a braid, a dagger in their belt and their thicker clothes and decided not to. But he did think about it.

"Perhaps you could just come with us and wander, hoping to bump into Iori Llew then."

Again he had a long think and declined, but asked them if they were anywhere near the new settlement, or saw Iori on their travels, to tell them he was alive and to come to visit.

The answer was that they never plan where they are going, they just wander, and don't like this area any more so are going much further afield. But if they had a chance to do it, they would.

So off they went, and he wondered if he would ever see them again, as theirs was a dangerous life.

Had he made a mistake in not going with them? He made the decision to stay for two more weeks. That would give some time in case the outsiders happened to meet up with Iori, and he would come to see him. He didn't think that would happen but you never knew. It was going to be a dangerous few weeks.

CHAPTER FORTY

THE KENNELS

That night he saw the signal in the window, and after putting on a special grass-coloured top scented by honeysuckle petals, he avoided the dog and especially the rats and got into the house after a nerve-wracking journey. He thought Gwyn would be excited to see him. Once again, however, all he talked about was Aled. He told him about the rats, and Gwyn said that his mam had seen them, and was scared to go out at all, even if Karl wasn't there. She knew when he left as his truck made a horrible loud churning noise and belted out clouds of dense black smoke. He told Egryn that she had told next door not to dump anymore but they ignored her as usual. His dad was phoning the council in the morning.

He also asked him about the new houses being built just down the road, and Gwyn confirmed the news and said the first ones were finished and people were moving in already. Even better news, Aled's family were moving into one of them, as having visited here and seen Ryan's family they decided not to put an offer in for the empty house next to them, which they were thinking of doing.

A few days later the council came to clear the rubbish, and fined Ryan's dad, but no sooner had they gone than he started dumping again. Egryn was seeing less and less of Gwyn. That weekend, Aled was moving into his new house which would be much nearer, so probably Gwyn would be spending even less time with Egryn.

Gwyn's parents were not happy at all living next door to Ryan's family as the dad was now enjoying himself shooting at the rats from his upstairs bedroom window and anything else that moved in the trees, including birds.

Egryn had to be very careful not to make any movement whilst moving along the branches. He already had one narrow escape when a small branch he was walking along rocked, and a bullet was fired and just missed him. He had to move much slower, especially if the branch was in view of Ryan's house.

Ryan was back to his bullying ways, and if Gwyn was playing in the garden he would climb over the fence and pinch his new ball or steal his toys. It was no good his parents complaining, as they didn't listen. One day Egryn saw Huw, Gwyn's dad, making his way to Ryan's doorway. Before he even knocked to make his complaints he saw the door burst open and Huw was told to get back to his own garden or he would get a punch on his hooter (nose) and the dog would be set on him to bite a hole in his bum. Huw skidaddled back like a bull out of a gate.

Gwyn hardly came out to play any more, and Egryn found it very difficult to get in and out of the house.

He wondered whether Iori Llew would come to see him after all. He hadn't so far but he might have been on his travels and possibly hadn't heard he was still alive. Or they had moved a long way away to a new settlement and Iwan and Gruffydd hasn't seen him and told him. *He probably doesn't know I'm alive*, Egryn thought.

What should he do? Go to find Iori Llew now, wherever he was, or try and find the outsiders? Perhaps it really was a mistake not going with them. Both ideas were very dangerous. Probably best to stay there a bit longer and wait to see if Iori Llew came. It was such a difficult decision, one he didn't want to make. He was really too scared to go off wandering on his own. But he was also almost too scared to go into Gwyn's house or search for food in the woods.

That Sunday things got much worse, if that was possible. Ryan's cousin and his family, four children and two adults moved in the house next door. They never told Gwyn's family and the first they knew of it was when the truck full of old furniture pulled up and started unloading. They looked even rougher than Ryan's lot.

That night after they had moved most of their furniture and junk in, they went into the woods and chopped down lots of branches and made a massive bonfire. Trays of cans of beer were brought out, and a music centre blasted out a horrible noise you could hear in the next village.

Egryn was scared stiff and fed up. Gwyn had forgotten all about him for the last few days, anyway it was too dangerous for either to go into the garden. He couldn't stand another day cooped up in his tree dodging flames or bullets, so he made his way very carefully to Gwyn's house.

He spent the night sleeping or at least trying to in Gwyn's bedroom, but he kept peeping out to check whether his tree had burnt down. Gwyn was glad to see him, because Aled had gone to his cousin's party. But things were not the same as before.

The next morning Gwyn went out to school and Egryn stayed in his room all day. When his mam suddenly came in to tidy his room, Egryn quickly hid down in the gap between the bed and curtain. Unfortunately just before she left the room, at the last minute, she pushed the bed further in towards the wall. Egryn was squashed tight and couldn't move. He could hardly breathe and kept fainting, he shoved but the bed was far too heavy. The hours seemed like days and he kept passing out, but was abruptly woken by the noise of a lot of dogs barking.

Breathing in and making himself thinner, he managed to move a few inches and his breathing got easier. It took him two hours to finally get to the end of the bed, he lay down on the carpet and fell asleep exhausted.

What he didn't know was Gwyn's mam came in to put some clothes she had ironed in his drawer, and she miraculously never saw him, probably because her hands were full. Not long after, Gwyn was back from school, came in and saw him, picked him up and placed him on the bed, then nipped downstairs for some milk for him. As he dabbed his lips with it, Egryn woke up and told him about being trapped and having a terrible dream about a pack of dogs.

It wasn't a dream. Gwyn told him to look out of the window. In the garden two doors away were four big wooden sheds.

"Those are kennels, just been put up. They've got eight dogs living in them now," explained Gwyn.

This was the last straw for his mam, who said they couldn't live there any longer. His dad was going to the estate agents tomorrow and was putting their house on the market.

Egryn stayed the night and when Gwyn went to school, he made his way back to his tree very carefully, still smelling smoke, and found it hadn't burnt down but a few leaves had been blackened.

When Gwyn came home from school his shirt was ripped, and he was very upset. Ryan's four cousins were all in the same school and they now had a gang on the yard and forced everyone to hand over any goodies they had. Aled, who was now in his school, refused, and they punched him in the face and grabbed Gwyn who tried to help him, and ripped his shirt.

When the teachers found out they kept the five of them behind after school and informed the parents. When they got back to the house, Ryan's dad stormed into Gwyn's garden, pushed open his front door, and shouted at Gwyn's parents that their son was a great big baby bunting and if they complained again, he would punch them as well. Seeing as he also had a gun in his hand, his dad thought it better not to say anything.

Next morning Gwyn didn't go to school. Instead his mam packed a suitcase and carried it into the car. His dad came out and did the same. Gwyn, before getting in, asked if he was going to school.

His mam said that she had decided temporarily to go and live in her mam's house and probably would enrol Gwyn in a new school, if there was room. His dad, before leaving for work with them, made sure the "For Sale" sign was up and pushed it in the ground a bit more before they drove off.

CHAPTER FORTY-ONE

THE GUNS

Egryn now was living in a terrible place. His friends and family were gone. Gwyn was gone. Most of the trees were gone. The pond was gone. There was no clearing any more. The squirrels were gone. The rats were back and bullets still whistled through the trees.

The nine dogs now wandered in and out of the gardens unsupervised all day. It was impossible for him to go on the ground at all. He wanted to leave but he was too scared to go on his own. He was too scared to even leave his tree when the gates were open, in case he was shot at, as the others had guns as well. At night they lined tin cans on the top of the fence and had a shooting competition. They often missed and bullets would whiz through the branches.

For the next two days, Gwyn's mam drove up to collect items from the house and Gwyn was with her, as he wasn't starting his new school until the beginning of next week.

While his mam was carrying stuff to put in the car she told Gwyn to pick up the empty beer cans which had been thrown onto their garden. This gave him an excuse to go near the tree where Egryn was, and he told him what was happening. He didn't know if he would ever see him again. He didn't have much time to say a lot as his mam wanted to spend as little time as possible next to that horrible lot.

Gwyn said if he wanted, whilst his mam was going back into the house for the last time, he would sneak Egryn into the car and he could come and live in his gran's house. He only had a few seconds to take all this in, and whilst he was pondering whether to or not, Gwyn's mam rushed out and told Gwyn to stop staring at that tree and jump in.

"The sooner we are out of this dump the better, let's hope I never have to come back here again!"

She didn't want to stay one more minute in this terrible place and got in and slammed the door, causing all the dogs to bark loudly. Egryn had hesitated, unsure, and then it was too late, the car was pulling away. Would he be back? Would he have another chance? Would he ever see him again? Everything had happened so quickly.

Two terrible days went by. Every night they had a fire, cooked meat on it and drank beer, played loud music and chopped more branches down. Still no sign of Iori Llew. Seems like the outsiders hadn't seen him.

He couldn't stay here any longer; he hated it. He couldn't go on the ground, his food was running low, rats were coming into his tree, guns were being fired at him, a pack of dogs were wandering around, Gwyn was gone, burning embers were blowing into the branches, the air smelt like a rubbish dump.

He collected some items he could carry including a few spare clothes and his precious catapult to set out immediately. After kissing all the oak trees that were left and saying goodbye to them, he made more journeys from tree to tree along the branches and landed as far away from the rats and dogs as possible. He didn't look back as he preferred to remember things like they used to be.

Which way should he go? He headed in the direction of the new settlement. He had been there once before, but was still careful going along hedges rather than open fields, checking for buzzards and red kites. It was much riskier doing it on your own as you couldn't watch the ground, the tree or the sky at the same time.

The next field was plastered with buttercups and Egryn remembered how Iori, Rhiannon, Alis Hâf and himself used to play hide and seek, at this time of the year, in that very field. They dressed in yellow costumes Rhiannon had made especially, and it was really hard trying to find anyone. Great fun. If only those days would come back. A tear trickled down his cheek.

Finally getting there, he was disappointed to find the new settlement empty. As he had feared, he could see signs that his elves had once lived there but had obviously left. There was another settlement not far away but that was the same, and he went to the smaller third one but nobody was there either. It was getting dark so he slept in one of the trees, a bit strange but safe.

CHAPTER FORTY-TWO

A DANGEROUS FLIGHT

From now on it was all going to be new territory as he hadn't been in this area when he was with Selwyn. For three days, he wandered in different directions and each night returned to the deserted settlement. There were roads, houses and farms everywhere.

Lots of fir trees had been planted. Elves hated them, as no creatures could live in or under their branches, and they poisoned the streams. He didn't like the smell either. When he saw a fir tree wood, he knew they hadn't been in that direction. He couldn't see any possible new settlement sites.

He could see why they left as arogs were living near. Should he stay here or wander even further, as they'd obviously gone a long way away? It would mean sleeping in strange places as it would be too far to come back every day. Should he just leave and keep going?

Whilst trying to get to sleep he suddenly had a great idea. Why not make a kite like the one they flew before? Yes, it would be much quicker. So the next day he found a suitable leaf and got it up with difficulty to the top of a tree, and found a good launching spot. Waiting for the wind to be in the right direction, he got all his gear and sat on at the top of the leaf and pushed off. Selwyn, remember, was the pilot last time, so he was bit unsure how to guide it. After about 20 seconds the front dipped and it headed down straight towards the ground. He leant back and twisted and turned. Just before he crashed into the ground, it whirled around and he landed fairly gently in a pile of ferns. No good.

For two days he tried different leaves and sitting in different positions and each time he went a bit further. He was gradually getting the hang of it. Eventually he was off and this was the real thing. After travelling about 30 metres, he had difficulty trying to balance so he didn't drop, and at the same time scanned the ground for any sign of a settlement. In the distance he could see a bird circling around, it looked quite big, so better to avoid it. He tried to lean a little to the right to make the leaf turn a bit but it wasn't enough, the bird was circling ever nearer. To his horror he could see it was a red kite and noticed that it had spotted him and changed directions.

He moved forward to make the leaf drop, and it did, but the bird was getting nearer. Leaning as far forward as possible the speed of the drop increased, and the bird wasn't catching him. Unfortunately he was going too fast to stop, and he was heading straight towards a tree. He tried leaning back again and it worked, but not enough. His leaf scraped along the top branches, he fell off sideways and tumbled down through the thin branches and landed on his back, knocking the wind out of him. He passed out for a short while, enabling the bird to catch up.

It took the bird a few more seconds to land, and he stepped nearer to the elf lying prone on the ground. Egryn opened his eyes just in time and saw this sharp, curved beak coming towards him, just inches away. No time to get up, even if he could – he closed his eyes just as the beak opened inches from his face and realized this was the end. He was going to be killed by a red kite after all.

CHAPTER FORTY-THREE

END OF AN ERA

As his eyes were closed Egryn obviously couldn't see, but he could hear an enormous shriek as two arrows hit the red kite. He was nearly squashed as the dead bird flopped on top of him. The heavy weight was pressing against him, and he struggled to breathe. The weight was getting heavier; his breathing was getting shallower. He was to die after all, suffocated and squashed by a dead bird.

In the nick of time, he felt the weight move, and he could breathe a little bit. Gasping air, he felt the weight getting less. Opening his eyes, all he could see were red feathers moving slightly.

After what seemed ages, the last part of the bird dropped off him and he could see two elves bent over, staring at him. He was gasping for breath. The three of them never moved, they were all too busy getting air into their lungs.

Gradually they all moved, Egryn sat up and seconds later the two elves lifted their heads.

To his immense joy he recognized Iwan and Gruffydd.

The three of them huddled together and squeezed each other in a great big bear hug.

"Careful," piped Egryn, "my ribs are still hurting from the bird."

They dropped their arms, and all looked at each other and laughed out loud.

They told Egryn that he was really lucky as they were crossing the valley, and just before they entered a wood, Gruffydd turned his head and saw a red kite circling above. They were just going to get under the cover of the trees for safety, when they saw the bird stop circling and turn towards them. Thinking it had seen them they went in a little bit, but realized the bird was heading slightly to their left.

Wondering who was going to be the victim, they watched and noticed the bird suddenly increasing speed and swooping down about ten metres from them, heading for the next tree. When the bird was directly above them, and almost in the tree, they heard something fall, crashing through the leaves at the side of the tree, and had a shock when they saw it was an elf landing heavily on the ground.

They had only seconds to spare as the bird landed and strode towards the elf, and realized they had time for only one shot each with an arrow.

You know the rest, the arrows landed and the bird dropped on top with its beak about six inches from the elf. Only one second later would have been too late.

"We had to rush over as we thought you would be crushed," stated Iwan, "it was really hard pulling the bird off, and at first we didn't think we could do it. We heaved and heaved and gradually it moved a little bit at a time."

"We never knew it was you," Gruffydd informed him. "What are you doing out here?"

They moved back under the cover of the tree, away from the dead bird, and sat down, while Egryn told them all about the events in the old settlement.

It was a very sad account and they were not surprised he left. He should have done it sooner and come away with them, when they left last time.

Egryn then explained why he was on a leaf as he couldn't find the new settlement, and asked if they knew where it was.

They replied that when they went to tell Iori Llew that Egryn was alive, they found that they had all left, it was empty. Checking the ground for any clues to which direction they went, they discovered it was to the south-west, towards that little hill there.

"Before we decide anything let's have something to eat," Gruffydd remarked, "there's some mushrooms growing under the trees, over by there, we've been here before."

They decided that was a good idea, and whilst sitting down eating some Egryn inquired how they had bows and arrows. Iwan told him that they were thinking about making some for ages. "There are lots more buzzards and red kites in the area now, also as new arog houses and roads are being built everywhere, foxes are looking for new territories. Even worse, some arogs have started a mink farm, very dangerous animals, real killers, and some have escaped. There are lots of them now, even the rats run away from them. Therefore we needed a new weapon, so we created our own bows and arrows, and after a lot of practice have become quite good at using them."

Egryn reminded them that weapons were banned.

Iwan replied that the rules don't apply to them any more, as they are wild elves. Times had changed dramatically and he wouldn't be surprised if eventually all elves had weapons.

They told him it was too dangerous for him to go back to the house, and too dangerous for him to go on by himself. Why didn't he join them and become a wild elf?

He couldn't go on alone, couldn't go back, but didn't want to be a wild elf, so he made a decision.

"I tell you what, I will join you if you go towards the south-west, if we don't find my relatives and friends in the next week then I will become a wild elf like you two."

"Great decision," announced Iwan, "let's drink to that!"

Gruffydd pulled three wooden jugs out of his pack on his back, and filled them with some acorn beer he had in another bigger one. They lifted the mugs in the air, and each took a large swig. Iwan then announced a toast.

"To our new journey!"

They gulped it down, packed the jugs away and strode off into the distance, heading south-west.